MW00884118

CHOCOLATE KISSES

RIVER FORD

Dee,
Chocolate and Kisses
make everything better.
River Ford

Fidem Press

Chocolate Kisses

ISBN: 1545573603

ISBN-13: 978-1545573600

Edited by Amie McCracken

Cover Design by SelfPubBookCovers.com/RLSather

❀ Created with Vellum

For Matt and Carmen

1

Eureka Springs, Arkansas

erri Manning sighed in relief when they turned down Spring Street. Her knees and hips ached from sitting for the last hour, and she couldn't wait to see her mom.

"Almost there, sweet pea." Her dad, Ken Manning, patted her hand. He hadn't called her by that nickname in years, and she found it comforting to hear now. "Your momma's been looking forward to getting you home."

She appreciated his attempt to keep things light and positive, but the truth remained. She was returning home in defeat. Her dad had driven down to Fayetteville to bring her home from the University of Arkansas with only one semester left until graduation. For the last year and a half she'd been exhausted and achy without knowing why. The doctors ran test after test trying to figure things out while she suffered through her day to day life.

Finally, a little before fall semester started, she got a diagnosis. She still hadn't recovered from the shock. Even though she had pushed her way through one more semester, she couldn't handle the constant pain, exhaustion, and the pressure of school anymore. It made it next to impossible to attend classes and pay attention.

They pulled into the drive. Kerri prepared herself mentally for the task of unloading her belongings and carrying them up the stairs to her room. *You can do this.*

Her dad popped the trunk. Kerri opened the back door and hauled out her suitcase. She was halfway to the porch when her mom ran out and pulled her into a hug. Even though the January weather was mild, her mom's warmth was exactly what she needed.

"Finally! I was getting worried." Cheryl Manning squeezed her tighter.

"Sorry. I asked Daddy to stop in Rogers so I could stretch and get some hot chocolate." She dropped the bag and clung to her mom.

"Good. There's nothing like cocoa with—" she paused expectantly.

"Extra whipped cream." Kerri finished with her mom's motto. "It's good to be home."

"Why didn't that man of yours drive you home?"

Kerri finally backed out of her mom's arms. "He had more important things to do."

"Nonsense! I'll have a good talk with him next time."

"We broke up." She kept waiting to feel devastated about her ex-boyfriend Steven, but she'd only suffered mild sadness to this point. She wondered if it was shock. Surely the man she'd spent two years with should have garnered a stronger response?

"Why?" Cheryl's brow rose.

"He...he didn't want to be stuck with my problems."

Kerri chewed on her bottom lip but stopped short of twirling her hair around her finger.

Her mom gasped. "He didn't say that did he?"

"Yes." Kerri reached for the suitcase, determined not to revisit her last conversation with Steven. "I really don't want to talk about it."

"Okay, but I'm here when you do. Come on, I've got your room all ready." Cheryl took the suitcase from her and walked through the front door. "I hope you don't mind, but we're putting you in the downstairs guest room. It's got its own bathroom and you won't have to climb the stairs."

Kerri swallowed the lump in her throat. Her family had made changes for her. Would her disease affect everyone she met? She felt so tired all of a sudden. Her body had become the cement block that would pull her to the bottom of the lake, never to surface again.

"Kerri?" Her mom touched her shoulder. "Is that okay?"

"Yeah. Thanks," she nodded.

"Well, go on and make yourself comfortable. Oh, and I saw Jaya the other day. She's back in town with her fiancé."

"Really? I didn't know she was coming home so early. I bet she's working on wedding stuff. I'll have to give her a call sometime." Kerri didn't want to think about her high school classmate's upcoming nuptials. Was it jealousy, or just regret? If she hadn't gotten sick, would she still be with Steven planning a wedding some time after graduation? *It doesn't matter, get over it.*

Kerri had to admit she was more in love with the idea of marriage and stability than she ever had been with Steven. In fact, she could now admit she'd never dated a guy that she missed after he left. She looked around the room in an effort to stop dwelling on the pathetic state of her love life. Her mother had redecorated the guest suite. The room had a fresh coat of pale blue paint that matched the tiny flowers in the quilt on the bed. The furniture was her grandma's cedar set. The rich red wood streaked with lighter stripes had filled this room for most of her twenty-three years. The scent had grown faint over the decades, but if she pressed her nose close she could still smell it.

A large, rounded mirror hung over the dresser. The two bedside tables had brass lamps with fringe-ringed shades on top of lace doilies. It wasn't that her parents were old fashioned, they just believed in using things until they stopped working. They rarely threw anything away. It was comforting in a way.

Her dad returned with another box from the trunk. He set it on the foot of the bed and sat beside her. "Come on, sweet pea. Chin up. Remember what the doctor said. A good attitude will go a long way in keeping this beast under control."

Kerri sighed and leaned over to rest her head on his shoulder, content to be his little girl for the moment. "I know, Daddy, but I feel like my life has ground to a halt. What am I supposed to do?"

He shifted to wrap his arms around her. "Maybe this is God's way of telling you to look for new dreams."

She groaned.

"No, hear me out. You went to school and changed a lot of things. What you wanted to do, where you wanted to live. Every time you came home I wondered what had happened to my baby. Perhaps this will help you find that carefree, happy girl again."

She wiped at tears. "I don't know where to start. I think I'm too scared to hope for anything."

"Ah, sweet pea." He squeezed her tighter. "Your mom

4

and I will hope for you until you can do it on your own again."

"I missed you calling me sweet pea."

He chuckled. "I'll forget your name is Kerri if that'll help you feel better."

"It just might." Coming home always made her feel better, and maybe her dad was right. She needed to find out who she was again.

Her phone rang as her dad stood. "That's my cue to grab some more stuff."

"I'll help if you give me a minute." Kerri's nerves rumbled. *Please don't be Jaya.* She searched in her purse for her cell, relieved to see her roommate Jen's face smiling up at her. "It's Jen."

"That didn't take long. You only left a few hours ago. Tell her I said hi." He closed the door behind him.

"Hey, I just got home." Kerri leaned back on the bed, enjoying the way it felt to stretch out.

Jen had been her best friend for as long as she could remember. The two of them, along with Jaya, Mic, and Brynn had survived high school together. However, Jen was the only one Kerri had roomed with at U of A.

"It's already lonely here." Jen tried to sound pouty, but she was one of those perpetually happy people. It's one of the things Kerri loved about her. "Guess what?"

"What?"

"I'm coming home in three weeks!" Jen screamed into the phone.

"What? How did you get off work?" Kerri couldn't believe it. Jen was always working. It's actually how they moved from friends to besties. When they were in middle school, Jen didn't have any money for candy or sodas, so they started their own cookie business. They never got rich, but they both learned to work hard. "Wait, why are you coming home in the middle of the semester?"

"In a minute. I have a favor to ask you." Jen paused and Kerri could hear her tapping her fingers on something.

"Why do I get the feeling I'm not going to like this?"

The fingernails on the other side of the line quieted. "Because you're probably not, but I want you to think about it."

"Uh-oh. Okay, spit it out." Kerri felt a wave of tiredness wash over her, but she knew if she could help her friend she would. Jen never asked for anything too hard anyway.

"I'm coming home Valentine's weekend." Another pause that lasted longer than normal. "For the chocolate festival."

"Oh." A spike of excitement jolted through Kerri before fizzling out. She hadn't thought about the chocolate contest since Steven had laughed at her over it. That memory haunted her as much as the pain that never really went away. "I don't know Jen. Working the chocolate might be too hard for me. Remember how much it hurt at Christmas."

"Come on, girl. Remember, use it or lose it. Even if it hurts, it could help. Don't give up. Just think about it. Plus, without the cost of school, you can afford all the medicine, right?"

"I'm still paying for school. My classes will just be online instead of on campus."

"Oh yeah." Jen paused before bouncing back even peppier than before. "At least we can still graduate together. You'll come back for that, right?"

"Yes, I wouldn't miss it."

"Good. Well, you've probably got a lot of unpacking, so I'll let you go, but promise me you'll think about it for more than five minutes?"

"I promise, but don't get your hopes up."

New York City

*E*ric Hunt hid by the catering door, watching the crowd mingle. They laughed, toasted his success. Few of them looked at the sculptures on display. They were more interested in being seen than seeing. He should have been used to it by now, but even two years in New York City hadn't erased his fond memories of gatherings at home. Life had been different there. More relaxed, and he knew who his true friends were. *Don't be the country boy tonight.*

He turned his thoughts to his latest work and cringed. The only thing he could say about the sculptures was they were larger than life. That's what his agent, Candace, had wanted. A statement as big as New York City. The twelve pieces on display represented various aspects of the Big Apple. The largest of the series filled the middle of the room. Skyscrapers grew upward and outward in a skewed version of a skyline. The buildings were larger at the top than the bottom. The details were good. He even had the illusion of people behind the windows, but it didn't make him feel anything. None of these city pieces did.

A glance at his watch showed half past eleven. Perhaps he could slip away without causing too much ruckus.

"Eric, there you are." A perfectly manicured hand brushed his arm. Long blonde hair draped over bare shoulders. The dress was practically sewn onto the woman's body. "I've been looking everywhere for you."

"What do you need, Candace?" He didn't move from his spot even though she tried to pull him into the open room.

"I need you…" She fluttered her eyelashes.

It took all he had not to roll his eyes. Candace wasn't the

biggest fake in his life, but she ranked pretty high. She was a great agent, but she flirted constantly. Eric never knew whether to take her seriously or not.

He felt the same about most of the women he'd met since gaining a bit of fame. They all flirted. Said they wanted him, but they only wanted their picture in the papers. They wanted to know who he knew, who could help them with their ambitions. He had learned his lesson the hard way, and even if Candace hadn't been his agent, he wouldn't give her the chance to break his heart like Vanessa.

"We agreed to keep things strictly business." He nodded toward the room.

"You're no fun." She waved toward the gathering with a small pout. "Come out and be seen at least."

She tugged on his arm again. This time he walked with her toward the middle of the gallery and his artistic interpretation of the New York City skyline. Photographers surged toward them. The staccato of flashes nearly blinded him.

"Try to look happy," she whispered.

Her beauty-queen smile was in full force for the cameras. The games women played for attention pushed him over the edge. He didn't care if she was his agent, he was done.

Eric held up his hand. "Everyone, thank you for coming tonight. I hope you've enjoyed the exhibit. Please excuse me. I have another engagement to attend tonight."

He retreated toward the door, Candace still clinging to his arm.

"That's not going to help you sell anything. Where are we headed?" her sickly sweet voice grated on his nerves.

Eric paused long enough to pry her fingers loose. "I need

some time alone. Find my creative vibe again. Get started on the next set of show pieces."

"So there isn't another place you have to be? Looks like I'm finally turning you into one of us. I'll let you get away with it tonight." She ran her finger down his tailored shirt and stepped closer. "Especially, if you let me help you with your creativity."

"Seriously, back off. Do I need to find another agent?" He turned his back on her and grabbed his coat and gloves from the valet.

"You're stuck with me until our contract is up." She dropped the sweet tone. "And trust me, if you try to get out of it, I'll slap you with so many lawyers you'll never find that vibe again."

Eric bristled but knew he had to keep calm. "I don't want out of our contract. I simply want you to be my agent and stop all this flirting."

"Why didn't you just say so?"

Eric rolled his eyes and walked out to the busy street. The temperature hovered just below freezing. The wind bit into his face, and he pulled the scarf up higher, covering his mouth and nose. At least it wasn't sleeting. Snow from the day before crunched under his feet as he hailed a cab.

"308 Mott Street in SoHo, please." Eric settled in the back and rubbed his hands together.

New York blazed with lights. Traffic was the only thing that moved slowly here. When Eric had first come to the city he had been dazzled by it all. Everything had been exciting. Now he just saw the dirty snow piled along the side of the street. It was starting to affect his art.

"Maybe it's time I get out of here," he mumbled to himself.

"What's that?" the cabbie asked.

"Nothing."

Once he settled in the apartment, Eric opened his laptop and Googled artist communities in the US. He scanned a list of websites. There were lots of up-and-coming cities, but he was sick of the run around. He wanted something quiet. Somewhere he could hide from his fake friends and work on creating art again.

"Top twenty-five small cities for art." He clicked the link and skipped the top ten entirely. "Eleven—Corning, New York. Too close. Twelve—Eureka Springs, Arkansas. Thirteen—" His gaze went back to number twelve. "Arkansas? They have art communities in Arkansas? You can't get any more remote than that."

2

*A*fter a week, Kerri's life fell into a new routine. Sleep, study, email her assignments, then head to the store to help her mother. She had successfully avoided most of her family and friends. Even Mic, although she didn't think that would last much longer, since she was the only one of their group that would cook with him. However, the thought of smiling and acting happy for all of them weighed her down. It wasn't fair they still had their whole lives in front of them—jobs they loved and relationships that could lead somewhere like weddings and babies. She had no idea what her future held.

Nothing. There's nothing.

Thursday morning, Kerri sighed and got out of bed. Her body ached and complained about every move she made. She needed to email a paper to her professor by nine o'clock, but she would soak in a hot bath first. She was grateful her teachers were willing to help her graduate on time, but typing made her wrists hurt and put her in a bad mood. It was a hundred times worse in the morning when she already felt like a zombie.

When she finished her homework for the day, Kerri grabbed her coat and walked down the hill to the family store. Dr. Dahler had told her to walk as much as possible to keep her knees healthy. He'd been her doctor all her life, and now he would help her survive this new challenge.

She lived a mile and a half from the shop. On a good day, it only took twenty minutes to walk down the steep streets. Kerri's family owned a little place on Spring Street selling handmade jewelry and beads. Mostly beads. Thousands and thousands of colored beads of every shape and size imaginable filled boxes and trays along the walls of the narrow shop. She used to help her mom make dangly earrings and necklaces to sell.

"Hey Mom. What do you need me to do today?" she nodded to her mother who sat behind the counter.

"Take over here so I can work on the Mardi Gras stuff."

"No problem." Kerri took her place and switched on a small space heater behind the cash register. Hours passed. She greeted customers, but mostly she huddled behind the counter trying not to think. Her mother returned after a while.

"You're sulking again. If you don't want to be here, do something else." Her mom shooed her off the chair.

"Like what?" Kerri rolled her shoulders and flexed her hands. The dull ache hadn't left her alone today.

"If you won't visit Jaya, call Mic or someone."

Kerri made a face.

Her mom wisely ignored it. "If you won't be social, at least get in touch with your creative side."

Kerri headed for the back room. It was a five by five space as familiar to her as anywhere in the world. She took a moment and breathed it in. The building was old and this room really showed the age. The paint peeled in the corners

12

and the floor dipped in the middle. Nothing could hide that old dusty smell either. She didn't know if it was in the wood or the threadbare carpet, but she had missed it.

She ran her hand along the high-back wooden chair that sat by a bench built into the back wall. As a teen she'd hated the stiff slats even when she loved making jewelry. Now she slid into the seat and allowed herself to appreciate how straight it made her sit. That was supposed to be good for her, but making jewelry would have her slouched forward in no time.

"Do it anyway." She whispered, pulling strength from the familiar surroundings.

The Eureka Springs Mardi Gras celebration needed quality necklaces. They couldn't have any of that cheap plastic junk for the royal court. She opened a box of bright pink beads and another one full of silver antiqued ones. It was time to take back her life and find something to make her happy.

~

*A*fter driving the length of Eureka Springs on Highway 62, Eric turned around and returned to Main Street and the Historic Downtown area. The artist in him thrilled at the way the streets climbed their way up the hillside. The buildings had character, history. Old brick, faded advertisements. It had the opposite effect on him as the steel and glass he'd grown accustomed to in the city.

He pulled into one of the public parking lots and squeezed a few bills into the payment booth. The weather was mild for the last day of January but cool enough he was grateful for his coat and gloves. He decided to browse the shops along Spring Street to get a feel for the community.

There were all kinds of things being sold—Christmas stuff, quilts, wind chimes of every size and variety you could imagine, an art gallery, handmade soaps, nuts, clothing, faeries, candles, and a decent sized bookstore.

The next shop was smaller than some of the others. Both sides were lined with tables loaded with bins of beads, and the middle had a display of tools and other gadgets needed to make jewelry. He was about to turn around and walk out when a dark-haired woman, with a touch of gray sprinkled throughout, called to him from behind the counter.

"Hello, welcome to Beads and Baubles. Are you looking for anything specific?"

Before he could answer, he heard a thump followed by a clatter and the sound of something spilling. An angry mumbling ensued. The woman at the register jumped up and hurried to the back corner of the store. It took her less than ten steps the place was so small.

"Are you okay?" she asked the person entering from a side room. The second woman knelt to the floor.

"Yes." Her angry voice drifted to him.

The air fairly crackled with tension. Eric hovered just inside the door, not sure if he should help or leave them alone.

"Don't worry about it." The first woman tried to help. "Let me do it. Why don't you go get some air?"

The second woman stood, giving Eric his first real glimpse of her. Her profile showed the same delicate bone structure as the first woman. She also had smooth skin, and hair a shade darker than the woman who had welcomed him. Soft curls fell around her shoulders. She wore a dark green sweater, a couple sizes too big for her slender frame, that reached almost to her knees where thick striped tights covered her legs. None of the women he knew would be caught dead in those bright leggings or the loose sweater. This woman wouldn't know a Versace from a Dior.

"Let me clean it up." Her voice softened but carried a bite of frustration.

Eric crossed the store, pulled forward by the need to see her closer. Her bone structure would be amazing to sculpt. The woman spun around when he cleared his throat. He came face to face with the most amazing brown eyes. They glittered with unshed tears. The rest of her countenance was open and expressive. Everything about her screamed real.

She sucked in a shuddering breath. "Oh!"

"Hi, can I help?" He felt a surprising need to comfort the fragile looking girl in front of him. She had to be close to his age, but the wide eyes that sparkled in the light made her appear younger.

She blinked a few times and rubbed her wrist.

"It's just beads." She glanced up through her lashes.

Attraction shot straight through him. She looked like a broken angel. That one simple look through misty eyes made him want to scoop her up and hold her until her wings healed. Eric directed his gaze to the floor, surprised at the effect one vulnerable expression had on him. He hadn't felt this way since Vanessa had left him. It took a moment to focus on the pink and silver dots. "Well, an extra pair of hands couldn't hurt."

"What?" She squeaked and glared at the older woman. "Does he know?"

"Know what?" Eric took a step back.

"Of course not. He just walked in. Believe it or not, I don't know him." The older woman stood up and held out her hand. "Sorry. I'm Cheryl and this is my daughter Kerri.

She thinks I'm a busy body determined to set her up with every available man in town. Are you?"

"Am I what?"

"Available?" Cheryl asked.

"Mom!" Kerri turned almost as pink as the beads in her hand. She looked at Eric with those big eyes, dropped the beads, and hurried toward the door.

"Kerri, wait," her mom called after her, but she had already fled. "I'm sorry. You must think I'm horrible, but I was only trying to make her smile. I didn't think she'd take me seriously."

Eric wondered why spilling a few beads would make a grown woman freak out. "Will she be okay?"

Cheryl nodded once, then shook her head. "No, she didn't take her coat. The cold will probably make her joints hurt worse."

He watched her put the beads in a box and walk to the counter. A thick wool coat hung on the chair behind it. It seemed a bit excessive for the mild weather outside. The day had leveled out around forty-five, but the wind was chilly.

"I'm sorry, I'll have to close up so I can take this to her."

"I could do it." Eric bit down on his tongue too late. What was he thinking? He'd only been in town an hour and he was offering to chase some girl through the streets. She was beautiful, but from the look of things she was a drama queen. That was the last thing he needed.

"What was your name?" Cheryl asked.

"Eric Hunt. I'm staying at the Grand Central Hotel." He held out his hand to shake hers.

"Billy can keep an eye on you." She nodded and handed him the coat instead. "She probably went up the street to Frank's store. He's at the top of the hill. Head on up, around the corner, and then he'll be on the right-hand side. If you get to the post office you've gone too far."

"Top, right. What kind of store?"

"He's a sculptor. Kerri loves it there."

"Really? So am I." Eric thought it strange she would trust a stranger to look for her daughter. "Are you sure about this?"

"I have a good feeling about you. Plus, we know all the shop owners between here and Frank's. I've got eyes everywhere."

"Sure." Eric wanted to make sure she knew she could trust him. "If it makes you feel better, you can look me up online."

"I think I will." The woman smiled and shooed him out the door. "Go on. I'll see you when you bring her back."

$\approx$

*K*erri's heart pounded. Her emotions flew in multiple directions at once as she ran past shops on her way up the hill to Frank's. She was angry that her fingers had refused to work and embarrassed by the failure. Then she'd turned to see an amazing pair of aquamarine eyes staring at her. It was hard to name the sensation she'd experienced as she took in the rest of the man.

Something jittery had moved into her stomach when she met that gaze. He had the kindest eyes. Time had frozen. She was well on her way to getting lost in their depths when he offered to help. Those few words sounded like pity to her, and she'd put her foot in her mouth. Why did she always talk before thinking? Of course he didn't know about her problems, but she had overreacted and run away like a child.

So much for making a good impression.

She pushed the thought from her head. Why would she want to make a good impression anyway? Someone that gorgeous wouldn't be looking for her, even if she were healthy. He had that manicured Hollywood stubble going on, making him look like a GQ version of a lumberjack. One that wore designer jeans and polo sweaters. The kind that needed a beauty queen hanging off each arm.

Stupid men!

Her steps slowed and her body ached by the time she made it to the top of the hill. It only took a couple of minutes, but she hadn't run in months. Her hips and knees screamed at her. She stepped into Frank's shop. Instead of the traditional bell or wind chimes others had over their doors, Frank had placed a cowbell. It was one of the ways he had made this place his.

"Be with you in a minute," a voice called from the back.

"Frank?" She headed for his workroom.

"Kerri, is that you?" A white haired man in his late sixties poked his head around the door. "You're home." He gave her a big hug. "You're shivering. Where's your coat?"

"I left it at the shop. Do you still have that little space heater?"

It didn't take long for her to get cold, especially since she'd lost so much weight. Kerri had often huddled over the vents at school, soaking in the warmth after walking across campus. She tried to catch her breath while she waited for Frank. Running had moved the ache deep into her chest. Was this a new symptom? Or was she just out of shape?

Just breathe. She tried to calm herself, but every little thing made her worry something else was going wrong with her body.

Frank pulled a small heater from under a table and

plugged it in. "Why haven't you been up to see me yet?"

Kerri sat on the floor and let the heat seep in. The tears she thought she had under control threatened to spill over again, making it even harder to breathe normally. *Get a grip!*

"Hey now, what's going on?" Frank patted her shoulder. "Mic was in yesterday and said you've been avoiding him too."

The bell over the shop door clanged again.

"Kerri?" a male voice called her name.

"Back here," Frank answered for her.

The stranger appeared in the doorway. Kerri couldn't believe he'd followed her. Maybe he really did think she was incapable of taking care of herself. It hurt more than she thought it should. Why couldn't she start over and make a better impression?

She took the time to look him over again. His brown hair had a little wave to it and curled around his ears. Her eyes were drawn to his hands. They looked strong and capable clenching her coat. Her coat?

"That's mine," she blurted out and tried to stand. Her body didn't respond but sort of flopped. She still sat, but now her arms were the only thing keeping her in that position. The run had been too much. Shame and embarrassment washed over her.

"Your mom asked me to bring it to you." He watched her carefully, his gaze full of something she didn't understand.

"I'm Frank." The older man held his hand out.

"Eric Hunt." He shook Frank's hand but kept glancing at Kerri. "I'm a sculptor too. Just came in today from New York City."

"Really? How do you know Kerri?"

"I don't. I mean, we just met and her mom wanted to make sure she got her coat."

Frank grunted and mumbled something about her mother before addressing Eric again. "Are you visiting or looking for a change?"

"A little of both." Eric shrugged.

Frank laughed and moved back to the piece he was working on. He chipped at the wood as he talked. "I came eighteen years ago for a change and never left. Life's simpler here. Slower. You have time to be yourself."

The words sank deep into Kerri's soul. They might have been aimed at Eric, but they were what she needed to hear. Her breathing eased. She pushed herself up a little higher and finally let go of the cold floor. Now she simply had to figure out who she was or who she could be with her prognosis.

"That's what I'm hoping." Eric smiled and a dimple appeared on his left cheek.

Kerri's stomach flipped. She could die of mortification. Here was an attractive man, with dimples no less, holding her coat, and she couldn't get off the floor. Perhaps if she sat still he'd forget she existed.

No such luck.

He turned that smile on her. The fluttery feeling threatened to explode right out of her. Seriously, she would throw up if he kept looking at her like that.

"Your mother was worried and sent me to find you." Eric extended his hand.

Heat crept up her neck. She shouldn't have run out on her mom, but looking weak in front of this man felt like the worst thing that had happened in a long time. Even worse than the time she started her period while on a school field trip unprepared. She'd hid in the bathroom until her mom could pick her up, but everyone knew what had happened. Mic called her Spot for months until Brynn made him stop.

"Kerri?" Frank stared at her. "Are you okay?"

She looked away from the two men standing over her to glare at the heater. "Yes, I'm just tired. I need to rest a minute before heading back to the shop."

Frank knelt beside her. "Honey, I don't understand."

"It's nothing." Her eyes flicked to the stranger. His gaze was glued to her, completely undoing any sense of peace she'd managed to gather. She had to put distance between the irrational hope those blue eyes pulled from her. There was one way to do that, but she couldn't bring herself to say the words. She focused on Frank and glossed over the problem instead. "Doctor Dahler figured out what's wrong. I just need to rest, and then I'll be okay."

"What did he say?" Frank asked.

"Can we talk about it some other time?" Every inch of Kerri's skin felt warm from Eric's gaze.

Frank glanced at Eric and nodded. "No worries, but let me help you up." Frank bent halfway down and winced.

"You'll throw your back out. Just give me some time." Kerri waved him away.

"I can help." Eric reached for her again.

Kerri sat on her hands. "No, really. I just need a minute."

"You're mom will think I kidnapped you." He bent down, slipped his arms under hers, and lifted her to her feet.

She stood in his embrace. Warm from head to toe. Her hands grasped his shoulders of their own will. The muscles of his arms felt solid under his shirt as her fingers skimmed downward to rest in the crooks of his elbows. The churning in her stomach turned into a cyclone. Trembling from the current running through her, she lifted her gaze from his chest to his eyes.

"Thank you," she whispered.

"Any time," he whispered back.

3

*E*ric pulled Kerri up without thinking. Her childish gesture of sitting on her hands confirmed his earlier suspicion she was overly dramatic. However, the moment her hidden curves settled into his arms, his heartbeat quickened. He liked the way she fit in his embrace— the way she checked him out by squeezing his muscles before she realized what she was doing. She was the perfect height for resting his chin on the top of her head. A deep breath proved she smelled incredible. Not a harsh perfume but some soft shampoo that hinted of vanilla or something.

She looked up at him, eyes wide, lips slightly parted. An uncommon sense of protectiveness ignited deep in his soul. He barely breathed, afraid she'd move away.

Frank coughed, and Eric realized he held Kerri closer than appropriate considering they'd just met. He tried to convince himself it was because she needed help, but he worried that wasn't it at all.

"Sorry." He let her go and took a step back.

"Well, then." Frank laughed. "I'll let Cheryl know you two are heading down the hill."

"Thanks." Kerri hugged the older man. "We can talk later."

Frank whispered something in her ear. She blushed and shook her head.

"Impossible."

The sadness in her voice tore at him. He'd have to be careful around her. Vanessa had been good at playing his emotions. Kerri didn't act as sophisticated as his ex-fiancee, but what did he know?

"We'll see." Frank nodded at him. "Let this young man bundle you up and take you home."

Eric didn't think it possible, but Kerri turned even pinker than before. It appeared as if every emotion she felt marched clearly across her pretty face. Each new expression sparked his imagination. Perhaps he could sculpt them as a series.

"I promise I don't bite." He didn't know why, but he couldn't resist teasing her. Something deep inside wanted to know how she'd react. Her eyes widened, and she looked everywhere but at him. Maybe she wasn't like the women he knew in New York. They would have smiled seductively and said something about hoping he did. He helped her into the coat.

Frank laughed again and walked them to the door. "Come visit me and we can talk shop, son."

"I'd like that." Eric led Kerri outside.

She seemed to shrink down into the long coat. Her hands gripped the front, holding it closed. Why didn't she button it? He thought about what her mother had said about the cold making her joints stiff. Maybe she couldn't button it? Did that have something to do with the doctor she'd mentioned?

"Need help?" He pointed to her coat.

Kerri squeezed her fists tighter and stared at the ground. After a moment her shoulders slumped. "Yes, please."

"Okay. No problem." Eric stepped in front of her. One by one he buttoned his way down the fabric. He wished he knew what she was thinking. Other women had asked for things, demanded his attention, but she acted embarrassed. That fact alone punched holes through the last of his emotional barriers. She didn't look at him once, but her lips pressed into a tight line. "Hey, you all right?"

Kerri nodded but didn't look up. Without thinking, he lifted her chin. Her soft skin contrasted the rough wool coat. In the afternoon light he noticed her burnt umber eyes had caramel colored flecks in them.

"We all need help sometime."

Her eyebrows shot up. "Do you need someone to button your coat like a three-year-old?" She waited half a second before retorting, "I didn't think so."

Eric glanced down, glad to see his coat was still unbuttoned. "Actually, I could use some help."

Kerri's eyes widened. She stared at his chest. Finally, a small laugh tumbled from her lips. It was light, almost musical.

"You're crazy." The second laugh was stronger. She took hold of the sides of his coat. Moving in slow motion, she wiggled the middle button through its matching hole, then one more above it. "That's all I can manage until I get my fingers warmed up."

"I can help with that." He tucked one of her hands between his arm and side while holding onto the other. "Let's get you back."

Her expression had turned serious again. Eric felt an urge to bring back her laugh. He couldn't help but wonder

24

what she'd been like before her diagnosis. Diagnosis of what though?

It's none of my business.

~

*K*erri's body felt stiff and uncooperative—in direct contrast with the antsy turmoil inside. She wanted to look into Eric's face again, but it was too dangerous. Something happened every time she did. Those eyes made her hope for things she had no right to want.

Someone to hold her. Love her.

The unwanted thoughts caused her to stumble. Eric held her tight and didn't let her fall. *Forget it, you have nothing to offer.*

She stared at his hands. They were large and just as strong as she thought they'd be. He hadn't put on gloves, and they were turning white with the wind, but they protected hers. It was a lovely gesture she shouldn't get used to. She tried to pull free, but he held tight.

"Your hands are getting cold." *Thank you Miss Obvious.*

"Better mine than yours." He smiled down at her.

How tall was he anyway? She wasn't tall, only five-foot-four, and her gaze was level with his chin.

Stop eyeing him, and put some distance between you. "We could put our hands in our pockets. Then we'd both be warm."

His lips tilted down and a little wrinkle appeared between his eyes. "True. We've reached your shop anyway." Eric let her go and opened the door.

The store was still empty of customers. Her mom walked over and hugged her.

"I'm sorry, Kerri. I didn't think you'd take my joke seriously." She backed away and smoothed Kerri's hair from her face. "Will you forgive me?"

"If you forgive me for overreacting."

Her mom tsked and waved her hand in the air. "Forgotten. Now what do you think we should do for this fine young man willing to bring you your coat?"

Kerri heard the barely contained glee in her mother's voice. "Mom—"

"Eric was it?" Cheryl turned to him. "You'll have to join us for dinner tonight. It's the least we can do."

"I'm sure he has more important things going on." Kerri felt her nerves skitter again, and hugged her stomach in an effort to calm them. She couldn't decide if she wanted him to say yes or no. She did know that her mom was up to no good.

Eric studied her. She hardly dared to breathe, but her lips turned up in a small smile. He smiled back.

"I wish I could, but I've got a meeting this afternoon."

Eric watched Kerri's face. Her smile dipped to a frown for half a moment before she pasted it back on. It no longer looked natural. She appeared vulnerable again, so hopeful and yet resigned. To what though?

Did she want him to come over? He decided the only way to know if Kerri was real or fake would be to spend more time with her. And he found that prospect exciting.

"Maybe I can join you for dinner tomorrow night?" He saw Cheryl's eyebrows lift. "It would be nice to hear your opinion on where this Realtor tries to stick me."

Cheryl laughed. "Everything is bearable unless they take you down a dirt road."

"No dirt roads then. What time should I join you, and may I have the address?" He pulled out his phone to put it in the GPS app.

"Nonsense! Your hotel is close and so is our house. We'll wait for you here. Trust me, you don't want to try parking on our narrow streets. Ken will take you back to your hotel afterward." Cheryl looked like the cat who'd caught the king of mice.

"Mom, maybe he'd rather drive." A look of panic crossed Kerri's face as she turned to Eric. "You really don't have to change your plans."

"Well, if he drives, you could go with him." Cheryl's smile grew wider. "You could help him find the best parking spot."

Eric watched the two women communicate through glares. Both were expressive and he tried not to laugh at the battle raging between them. He wanted the mother to win, so he decided to help her out.

"That would be great. I haven't been anywhere other than downtown yet."

Kerri rubbed her arms again. It looked like it was more than just a nervous gesture. Her brow furrowed. She looked up at him, and he struggled to keep from reaching for her. He'd only known her half an hour, and he was more mesmerized by her than any of the women he'd known in the city—even with the drama. That had to be a world record of some kind.

"What would you rather do? Ride with us, or me ride with you?" Kerri fumbled over the words.

"Whichever one makes you more comfortable." That earned him a real smile, at least one that felt real to him.

"Okay." She tilted her head to the side and considered him. "Since my dad's car takes up the only other parking spot at the house, why don't you ride with us. Then, if you'd like, I can teach you how to use the trolley while you're here.

It's limited this time of year, but it's a fun way to get around without worrying about parking."

"Does that mean you're taking me on a tour of Eureka Springs?" He glanced at Cheryl who'd been standing quietly. She had her fingers crossed.

"Maybe? How long are you staying in town?"

"A couple of months. My meeting is with a Realtor to find somewhere to rent."

"Oh, yeah. You just said that. I could show you around. We're closed on Wednesday if you can wait until next week." Kerri glanced at her mom. "Do you want to join us, Mom?"

Cheryl shook her head and moved to the register. "No thank you. I already have plans."

"What?" Kerri raised an eyebrow.

"Stuff. You'll have more fun without me anyway."

Eric almost choked in his effort not to laugh. His mom would love Cheryl. It seemed they both had a penchant for matchmaking in spite of threatening looks from their children.

He coughed to shove that thought from his head. His mother would never know about these two. This new start was about art, not finding a cute girl to date. "I've never been welcomed to town quite like this. Dinner tomorrow and touring on Wednesday."

"I can't believe you're going to make him wait almost a week. We aren't open on Sunday." Cheryl started fussing with random things on the checkout counter.

"Mom, I'd rather not plan anything for Sunday. When Jaya sees me at church, we'll probably have to get together."

"Oh, that's true."

"It's perfectly fine to wait until Wednesday." Eric wondered at the strangled tone in Kerri's voice. Who was this other person and why didn't she want to do anything with her? "I need to work, and it could be nice to view the town relative to where I find to rent."

"True." Cheryl stopped her fidgeting. "By the way, what made you decide to move here even though you've never seen the place?"

Eric chuckled in spite of himself.

"Mom."

"No, it's a valid question. Let's just say I needed to do something completely impulsive, and Eureka Springs grabbed my interest while I was doing internet searches." Eric moved toward the door. "I'll see both of you tomorrow night."

"Okay. We close at five." Kerri walked to the door with him. "Thanks for bringing the coat."

"Glad I could help." Eric lingered a moment too long before walking out the door.

He'd retrieve his rental, check into the hotel, and look at properties online before he met the Realtor. That would be exactly what he needed to get his mind off the lively brown eyes. However, he couldn't forget how Kerri's entire face lit up when she laughed. She was so beautiful it almost hurt. In fact, his fingers itched to touch her so he could memorize every detail to duplicate in clay. It was a welcome urge. Something he hadn't felt in months, and he didn't think looking at houses would change that.

4

$\mathcal{K}$erri found it hard to concentrate on her school work. Eric was coming for dinner. There was something about him that made her forget her problems. However, she couldn't decide if that was a good thing or not. Now wasn't the time to worry about it though. One day she might get her pain under control, then she could think about relationships.

She wiggled her fingers, hoping it would limber them up enough to finish her finance paper. It was just so boring. Maybe it would be okay to take a break and make something for after dinner. Something special. Plus, she owed it to Jen to see if her hands could handle making fondant and dipping chocolates. Jen had called twice in the last week, but Kerri still hadn't given her a solid yes or no.

Kerri had just finished cleaning the counters and getting all her ingredients out when someone knocked on the door. A momentary twinge ran through her. It might be Jaya and Aiden. She didn't know if she could handle their cute togetherness after the way Steven had left her. *Suck it up.*

It was time she talked to the rest of her friends about her problems. After the first meeting, everything would be fine. It had to be. She didn't realize she'd been holding her breath until it whooshed out at the sight of Mic. His blonde hair flopped everywhere, but he was exactly who she needed.

"Cosmo!" Kerri flung herself into his arms. "I missed you. Come in."

"Sure, Spot." He growled at her before giving his signature grin.

"Sorry, it slipped out. I promise not to call you Cosmo, if you'll do the same with Spot."

"I thought we'd agreed to that years ago." He slipped off his jacket and laid it across the top of the couch. "Why have you been hiding? Jaya and Brynn are both in town and they're worried you haven't called them."

"It's a long story. Want to join me while I make some treats?" Kerri led the way to the kitchen. Mic was an excellent cook and they often spent their time catching up while creating some confectionary treat or another.

"I'd love too." He walked straight to the sink to wash his hands. "Still got my extra apron?"

"Yep." Kerri opened the pantry and reached for the shelf hidden beneath the bottom of the larger shelf. They'd hot glued it there during their eighth grade school year. She pulled out the square of black fabric and handed it to Mic. "I can't guarantee it's been washed in the last four years, but here you go."

"Thank you much." He did a funny little flourish of a bow. "Now, I'm assuming you're making truffles?"

"How do you always know?" Kerri couldn't help but smile. Having Mic in her kitchen felt like old times. Better, happier times.

"Chef's instincts. Plus, I might have talked to Jen yesterday." He ducked when Kerri took a swing at him.

"What did she tell you?"

"Not much. Just that you probably really needed your friends right now." He sobered. "What's going on?"

Kerri placed heavy whipping cream, and her favorite dark chocolate in a saucepan and turned it on low. "Stir and I'll tell you."

"But stirring is your favorite part."

"I know. It hurts my wrists though." Kerri pulled up a stool and sat down. She flexed her fingers and rolled her wrists a few times. "Remember how I was complaining about always being sore?"

"Yeah. I remember Jen saying you even missed some classes because you were so tired all the time."

"Dr. Dahler ran some blood work before last August and it turns out my RA levels were sixty-four."

"I don't know what that means." He tipped the pan a little. "Is the butter ready?"

"Yes." Kerri handed him a smaller bowl with room temperature, whipped butter. Then she opened a jar of her mom's homemade raspberry jam. "Normal people have an RA level of around fourteen."

"Okay, that sounds bad then, but what's RA?"

"Sorry. It stands for rheumatoid arthritis. It's not the same kind of arthritis your grandma had."

"I'd hope not, you're too young for that." He kept stirring, his eyes a bit mischievous. "Are you going to smell like Bengay from now on?"

"It's not funny, Mic." She dropped the bowl with a clatter and waved the wooden spoon at him. "My immune system is attacking my joints. When the disease runs its course, I'll be one of those deformed people who can't use their hands anymore." The words rushed out as if she could no longer hold them in. Thinking of that future, the one where she would always be in pain and might not be able to walk or do anything for herself, brought the tears. "I'm in pain all the time, but no one can see it."

"I'm sorry." Mic set the pan to the side, away from the heat, and hurried to hug her. He really was the brother she'd never had but always wanted. "I don't know what to say."

Kerri cried on his shoulder and mumbled, "There's nothing to say. That's why I've avoided telling you and the others. There's nothing you can do about it, and I really didn't want you to feel sorry for me."

"Are you in pain now?" He squeezed her tight, which made her cry harder.

"All the time."

She could feel a hitch to Mic's breathing. Now she'd made him cry. "I'm sorry. I shouldn't have told you."

"Of course you should have. I'm your best friend, right?"

Kerri pulled away and wiped at her face. "Well, second best at least."

"Ouch, that hurts." Mic clutched at his chest in mock pain. Then the smile that had teased his lips fell away. "There has to be treatments, or something."

"There isn't really a cure, only ways to slow down the progression."

"What do we do to slow it down?"

She moved around Mic and added the butter to the chocolate mixture before spooning some of the jam into it. "I have to stay active. It's one of those 'use it or lose it' kind of things. Then there are pills, but the medicines are expensive."

"Have you tried the healing waters of Eureka Springs? I hear they can cure cancer, so they must be good for RA." Mic winked at her. It was just like him to joke about it and make her smile. Too bad the springs didn't have real magical qualities. She could go for a miracle about now.

Kerri laughed. It felt good to be able to joke about it with a friend. "Sure thing. Now pour this batch in that container over there." She pointed to the supplies she'd already laid out. "We'll make some peppermint and peanut butter ones too before we start dipping."

"Can I film us?"

"No! No business today. Let's keep this just you and me and fun. Just like old times."

"Okay, but you'd make a great guest on my vlog. I'd pull in more male viewers with a beauty like you."

"Shut up." Kerri slapped him on the arm. "Just get to work."

"Do I get to take half of them home with me?"

"Sure." Kerri watched him set the bowl aside to cool. Eventually, they'd scoop the mixture into balls, cool them in the fridge, and then dip them in more chocolate. "Doesn't Brynn like the raspberry ones?"

"How would I know?" Mic didn't return her stare.

"Whatever! I bet you remember the name of every guy she dated in high school."

"I remember the name of every guy you dated as well. What's your point?"

"Fine." Kerri knew Mic had crushed on Brynn since their junior year in high school. Brynn, however, had run away to Italy and ever since then all she did was brag about how big a star she was going to be. Truth was she could do it too. She had a beautiful voice and the drive it took to make things happen.

"Let's talk about something else." Mic washed out the pan and returned to the counter with it. "For instance, Frank said you met a new guy yesterday."

"Seriously? Are you over there every day?"

"No, but I passed his shop and he waved me in last night. Said there were some sparks flying between you and some guy from out of town. What's that all about?" He started the next batch of filling.

"Absolutely nothing. He's just some guy Mom sent up with my coat. I barely know Eric."

"Eric. Well, I'll see what I can find out about him."

"You don't have to. Mom invited him for dinner tonight." Kerri sighed before she realized what she was doing.

"Wait, are these for him? You're trying to impress him." It was Mic's turn to point a spoon at her. "Don't you have a boyfriend?"

"Ugh, we are not talking about Steven. Not today, not ever again."

"What happened? You know I'll get it out of you eventually."

"But not today." Kerri squeezed his arm. "We've had enough serious talk for the whole week, don't you think?"

"Probably, but you know you can talk anytime you need."

"Thanks, Mic. Now keep stirring."

The next few hours flew by. They melted, shaped, dipped, cooled, and finally decorated almost a hundred and fifty truffles. By the end, they were both tired but laughing. Kerri snuck away to take an extra Mobic, hoping it would keep the pain at bay. She didn't dare take the medicine that made her nauseous. It would be such a shame to have spent an entire day making something special for Eric and then have to cancel because she was too dizzy to stand.

Mic waited for her in the living room. He walked with her to the shop and then left to go make another video for his channel. She didn't know how he had done it, but he'd found a way to make money being himself. That's what she needed to do. Could that revolve around chocolate?

She wasn't sure, but she had enjoyed the morning immensely. Now she'd work a couple hours with her mom, and then it would be time for dinner with Eric Hunt. For a moment she let herself enjoy the prospect. Mic had teased her about Eric and told her she should go for it. It was fun, but she hadn't reminded Mic how hard that would be. He had already forgotten what her diagnosis meant for her future. She understood how it happened. She'd been normal all morning. Mic couldn't understand her invisible disease. Not yet.

One day he would. They'd all understand as her hands curled in on themselves, refusing to function.

~

Kerri glanced at the clock. It was almost five. She had spent the afternoon checking inventory. Since that hadn't taken long, she had tried to sweep. Her lower body still grumbled at her for running the day before, her hands ached from making chocolates, and now her shoulders and neck hurt too. Her meds couldn't fight it all.

Her mom wisely left her alone, but the silence was unbearable. She knew her dad would be home by now, starting dinner.

"Mom, did you let Daddy know we had company coming?"

Cheryl looked up from the necklace she was stringing. "Of course. He said you made chocolates this morning."

"Yeah, Jen asked me to think about the chocolate festival."

"Oh good. You should do it. Your dad said the house smells wonderful."

"What did you tell him exactly?" Kerri twisted her hands together and watched her mom try to hide a smile.

"Nothing dear, just that we met a new friend and invited him over."

"Mom?"

"Kerri, I promise I'm not doing anything more than being friendly." She paused and glanced at the clock. "However, I looked him up on the internet this morning, and I'm fine with you being friendly too, if you know what I mean."

Kerri groaned. "Seriously?"

She wasn't really upset with her mom. Eric was really nice to look at, and he seemed polite and considerate. However, she didn't have anything to offer in the way of relationships in spite of what Mic had said. Nothing but her moodiness, pain, and fear. Regret filled her until her mom's words sank in.

"Wait, you found him online?" She hurried to the computer they kept by the register.

Why hadn't she thought to look him up? She had barely clicked on the browser when the door opened and he walked in. His smile with that dimple made her as dizzy as some of her meds.

"Hi." She sat on the stool to catch her breath. Spending time with him really wasn't a good idea. She would get used to looking at him, and then what would she do when he left?

"Hope I'm not too early?" He walked closer and Kerri forgot how to talk.

Her mom appeared with two coats in hand. "You're just in time. Here's your coat, Kerri. I've already locked the back door. I'm going to help your dad. Turn out the lights and get the front door for me will you?"

"Yes ma'am." Kerri said it out of habit but blushed when Eric cocked his head to the side. He continued to stare. "What?"

"Nothing. It's just refreshing to hear someone say 'yes ma'am.' I don't think I've heard it since leaving home."

"Oh." Kerri shut down the computer and the register. She'd already balanced the day's sales with the till. "Where did you grow up?"

"North Carolina." He held her coat for her, pausing until she was safely inside. "Would you like me to button it for you?"

Kerri felt her cheeks warm. Not out of shame this time, but something else. He stood close enough for her to smell his aftershave. It was different from her dad's. A little stronger but in a nice way. It made her want to lean forward and breathe him in. She almost did before a new thought slammed into her.

"Mom left!"

Eric laughed. "Yeah, she said goodbye and everything."

"We were supposed to ride with her." Kerri rubbed her arm furiously. She knew her mom was up to no good. How had she let her get away with it?

Eric chuckled. "Your mom and my mom would get along great. Don't worry about it. I can get my rental and pick you up."

"You're not mad?"

"Why? She probably just forgot."

"Yeah, and I'm the next Willy Wonka."

"What?"

"Never mind." Kerri grabbed her purse and headed for the door. "Come on, I'll walk with you to your car."

Eric stepped out first and waited for her to lock up. When Kerri turned around, she almost bumped into him.

"Sorry." Kerri felt breathless again. He smelled really good.

"Let me help you. I'd hate for you to get too cold." He used her coat to pull her closer.

Kerri's heart kicked into overdrive. She stared into his eyes, wishing she could understand the look. Was he going to kiss her? He didn't even know her. She didn't know him. Why wasn't she scared? And, oh boy, she wanted him to kiss her.

The warmth from Eric's body protected her from the chilly night. One by one he buttoned her coat as they stood under the streetlamp. Each moment passed by agonizingly slowly. A sweet torture she couldn't comprehend. Steven had never affected her this way. She couldn't remember any boy or man making her feel like this.

Steven.

Memories of their last conversation flickered through her mind. All she'd wanted was for him to hold her. Tell her everything would be okay. That he loved her and wanted to make things better. Instead, he'd been distant and barely touched her. Finally he got the nerve to tell her they should call it quits because the RA changed things for him.

Reality pressed into Kerri's senses. She wasn't girlfriend material anymore, and she couldn't let this man think otherwise.

"I don't want a boyfriend," she blurted out.

"Okay." He stepped back, his brow wrinkled. Eric turned

and walked in the direction of Main Street and his hotel. "I'm not looking for a girlfriend, so we agree."

Kerri thought she would feel relieved, but she didn't. Filled with concern over that point, she almost missed the stairway shortcut. "If you're at the Grand Central, we can cut through here and get to Main Street faster."

5

*E*ric watched Kerri out of the corner of his eye. For a moment he thought she wanted him to kiss her. He had leaned forward just before she announced she didn't need a boyfriend. It stung. He hadn't been rejected like that in years. At least she wasn't chasing him for attention. That was a nice change. Or at least it should have been.

Still a little confused about his own emotions, he backed off. She looked fragile again. Alone and lost even though he stood beside her. Eric reached for her hand and squeezed it. Kerri looked up at him in surprise.

"Why did you do that?" she asked.

"You looked cold. Even friends hold hands sometimes. See, no strings attached." He lifted their hands to eye level.

It brought the smile he hoped for.

"Is that how it works in North Carolina?"

"Ah, so you were paying attention. We are raised to be gentlemen in the Carolinas. Sometimes it gets us into trouble though. Women think we're coming onto them when we're only being polite."

Kerri laughed. "Surely not every man from North Carolina is a gentleman."

"Probably not. Here's my car." Eric pulled out his keys and opened the passenger door to a sporty, red hard-topped convertible.

"Nice. A bit flashy don't you think?"

"It's a rental. You should always drive the best when you rent." He didn't bother to tell her it was his way of test driving it. He'd need to buy a car since he didn't plan on returning to New York.

Kerri directed him to her house where he squeezed in beside her mom's Camry. Unfortunately, he couldn't open his door wide enough to get out. Kerri opened her own door.

"No," Eric cried. "My gentleman card will be revoked."

She laughed. "Whatever, crawl out this side before dinner is too cold to be good."

He loved when she laughed. In order to hear it again, he made a big deal of crawling over the gearshift and falling out her door.

"How will my ego ever recover?" He laughed with her and got to his feet.

The front door opened, and Cheryl peeked out, a tall man with salt and pepper hair stood behind her.

The man called out, "Sweet pea, what's all the commotion out here?"

"Nothing, Daddy. Eric just parked too close to Mom's car." She giggled again. "That's my dad, Ken Manning."

Eric stepped onto the porch and shook the man's hand. "Nice to meet you, sir."

Ken looked him over before waving him inside. "Come in out of the cold. I'm hungry."

Eric waited for Kerri to walk in with her mom first. Out

42

of the corner of his eye, he saw Ken nod in approval. It reminded him how much he missed his own dad.

"Cheryl tells me you're a sculptor." Ken ushered him in and closed the door.

"Yes sir."

"Done anything I might have heard of?"

Eric shrugged. "Probably not. I just had a show in New York City. Most of the pieces sold, but I'm learning that doesn't mean they were any good."

Ken gave him a good-hearted slap on the back. "I like you. Honest and down to earth. Just like Cheryl said." He pointed down the hall. "Come into the kitchen with us. We're not too formal around here."

"I like that."

Kerri and her mom were already busy. The smell of fresh baked rolls filled the air. He noticed Kerri trying to tie on an apron. She fumbled with it and her brow furrowed. Her mom moved over and tied it without a word.

"Thanks." Kerri gave her a sad little smile.

Cheryl didn't say anything but squeezed her daughter's hand. Eric watched them move about the smallish kitchen in well-practiced movements. Everyone knew their part in the routine, and it worked well.

"What can I do to help?" he asked.

"Oh, you don't need to do anything." Cheryl waved a potholder at him. "You're our guest."

Kerri glanced his way, and he noticed a brightness in her eyes that hadn't been there at the store. She tipped her head to the side as she looked at him. "If you really want to do something you could set the table. Everything's almost ready."

"Okay, point me in the right direction." He followed her into the dining room where she opened a China hutch.

"It's all in here. We need plates and bowls."

Her hand brushed Eric's as she turned back to the kitchen. The awareness between them was different from anything he'd ever felt before. Time slowed as he fought the urge to reach out and stop her from walking away. Why did such a small thing feel so big? Kerri paused and looked over her shoulder. Her eyes intense. Did she feel it too?

The moment passed, and she scurried back to the kitchen. There was no doubt she felt the same connection when they touched. He only questioned why she ran from it.

By the time Eric finished setting the table, the Mannings had joined him in the dining room. He sat across the table from Kerri, enjoying the conversation that flowed naturally around him. Ken told him stories about the town and his time in the military. It was clear he adored Cheryl and Kerri and that they loved him just as much. The father-daughter interactions had Eric thinking of his own dad again. He had died of a heart attack several years earlier, and Eric still missed him as if it had been yesterday.

After dinner, Cheryl slipped away before returning with a plate of chocolates.

"Try one and tell me what you think." She put the tray beside him.

Closer inspection revealed a dozen perfectly formed truffles. There were dark, milk, and white chocolates drizzled with a variety of colored swirls. They looked too perfect to eat.

"What flavors are they?" He leaned closer, waiting to make a choice.

"The white chocolate ones are peppermint." Kerri reached across the table and pointed them out. "Dark chocolate raspberry and milk chocolate peanut butter."

"They all sound good. I'll try this one." He picked up the raspberry truffle and bit it in half. The firm outside cracked open and gave way to a creamy middle that practically melted on his tongue. The flavor wasn't overpowering but definitely raspberry. With a smile, he popped the other half in.

Kerri watched him. Her eyes intent, leaning forward as if her life depended on his reaction to the treats. Eric retrieved a peppermint truffle and repeated the tasting process. He'd been afraid the mint flavor would be too strong. However, like the raspberry, it was exactly right.

"These are some of the best chocolates I've ever eaten. Where did you get them?" He considered the peanut butter. If they were half as good as the first two, he might be tempted, but it had never been a favorite flavor so he took another raspberry.

"You really think they're good?" Kerri asked.

"The filling is perfect. Smooth, just the right amount of flavor. Trust me, a friend of mine loved chocolates and had me try every truffle in New York. At least that's how it felt." He didn't mention it had been for their wedding reception. Vanessa had decided not to marry him three days before the big day, so it didn't matter anyway. "These remind me of my mom's. She used to dream of becoming a world class chocolatier. Life didn't work out that way though."

Kerri sighed and relaxed in her chair. "I'd like to talk to your mom."

Cheryl laughed and sat down. "Do you think she'd understand you better than me?"

Eric could tell she was teasing, and not really hurt, because her eyes twinkled like her daughter's.

"Of course not, but I bet she could share some baking secrets with me." Kerri returned her mom's smile but

45

rubbed her arms. "And maybe her story would help me right now."

"Sweet pea, pass them over here." Ken looked at his daughter with such tenderness.

Thinking he meant the truffles, Eric passed the plate to him, but Ken reached for his daughter's hand instead.

"Daddy, you don't have to—" A blush crept up her cheeks.

"Nonsense. Give them here." He took one hand and started kneading her palm with his thumbs, working his way through each finger and up her wrist, then up her forearm.

Kerri's brow creased, and she closed her eyes for a moment.

"Too much?" Ken asked.

"No, it's helping." Kerri glanced at Eric and then stared at the table. "My arms hurt sometimes."

Her dad snorted.

"Daddy."

"Sorry, sweet pea. I couldn't help myself. You always did have a knack for understating things, but I understand." Ken switched hands but didn't say any more.

Eric didn't either. It was clear Kerri didn't want to elaborate. Fingers that didn't work right and arms that got sore. What was going on with her?

$\sim$

Kerri dared a peek at Eric. He looked so comfortable sitting at the table with her family. She could tell her dad liked him almost as much as her mom. That sent a dangerous thrill straight to her heart. Her dad always knew what she needed, just like now. Her hands and wrists ached so badly, but she didn't want to excuse herself yet. Not with such a charming guest.

Eric was staring at her again, even though he was talking to her mom. "Mrs. Manning, where did you get the chocolates?"

"You haven't figured it out yet? Kerri made them. She's always playing around with recipes, trying to find the perfect balance of flavor and decadence."

"She's really good at it." Eric's gaze slipped to Kerri's lips then back to her eyes.

Oh my! If he kept giving her looks like that she wouldn't need a heater to thaw out. Kerri looked at her hands, reminding herself he couldn't mean anything by it. He was only staying a few months and was way out of her league. She took a few deep breaths to calm her racing heart.

"What got you into chocolates?" Eric asked.

"My best friend Jen. When we were young she didn't have money to buy chocolate, so we decided I'd use my allowance to get the ingredients. We figured if we could make them to sell at school she'd get candy and money." Kerri had loved those days. They ate as much as they sold.

Her thoughts were interrupted by her mom's laughter. "You should have seen the mess those two made. Chocolate and powdered sugar everywhere. And the flavors! Ugh, I don't know where they came up with some of them."

"Hey, olive truffles could have been the rage if you'd given them half a chance." Kerri shrugged, trying not to laugh herself.

"But my sweet pea figured it out." Her dad squeezed both hands. "She still plays with flavors, but now each one of them is incredible."

"Not all of them, but thanks Daddy." Kerri blinked away the moisture that threatened. She could feel her dad's love in each word, and it made her feel so guilty. She hadn't *played* with flavors since leaving for college.

"Why don't you sell chocolates at your store?" Eric reached for another raspberry truffle. She noticed he hadn't tried the peanut butter ones.

"I've been away to college, and with the other chocolate store no one would want mine." Kerri tried not to sound like it was a big deal to her.

"Kerri used to dream of owning her own shop with Jenny. That's why she was studying business at school." Her mom stood and gathered the dirty plates.

"Used to?" Eric asked.

Kerri stared at the table while she helped her mom. She didn't want to talk about this again.

Her dad answered for her though. "She doesn't think she can now. I think its hogwash. My girl can do anything she wants."

"Daddy—" Kerri took the dishes from her mom. She needed a break from the crazy emotions. She didn't know if it was the medicine or just trying to get used to the changes RA had forced on her, but everything made her want to cry. Instead of making excuses, she headed to the kitchen.

Kerri let the warm water run over her lower arms before she rinsed the plates and loaded the dishwasher. The whole time she listened to the conversation in the other room.

"I think she should open a candy store, give that other place a run for their money. She could even sell them online. Ship them all over the country. All she needs is to get the word out." Eric sounded like he really believed that.

Her mom and dad talked about ways she could set up a kitchen and website. None of them seemed to notice she hadn't come back. Her earlier emotions drained away, leaving her empty. They talked about her future the same

48

way Steven had before they broke up—like it was a done deal without even asking her what she wanted.

Steven was the one who had put an end to her chocolate dreams. He had planned their entire life after only six months of dating. Get matching internships, graduate, get jobs in some big city, marry, and travel the world. Because of his plans, Jen switched her major from marketing to elementary education. Kerri had been fine with it all because she thought Steven loved her. Then he'd walked away without even a kiss goodbye.

I'm done letting other people plan my life for me. A little irritation flamed to life, but she knew she was all bluster and no bite. Her parents were dreaming for her. That's why she came home, because she couldn't deal with it on her own. She'd always need help, because she'd never be able to afford all the medicines she needed. This disease would march unchecked through her life. *Why couldn't I have the easy arthritis? The one managed by aspirin?*

"Honey, are you coming back?" Cheryl walked into the kitchen. "That young man is getting lonely in there."

"I doubt that." Kerri mumbled but dried her hands. "I'm just tired."

Eric stood in the doorway with the truffle plate in hand. The smile was gone. "I've stayed too long."

"Oh no! I'm sorry, I didn't mean to imply—" She hated the way he rattled her. He must think she was so rude. "I've enjoyed...it's just late. I'm usually asleep by now."

"By the fireplace." Her mom chimed in. "I don't know how she can stand the heat, but all week I've found her asleep just a few feet from the hearth. I worry she's going to catch fire."

Kerri watched Eric put the plate on the counter. He didn't look upset, just thoughtful. There was no way for him to know that sometimes the pain and exhaustion knocked her out. She wondered if she should tell him.

Why would he need to know? It's not like my life will affect his.

She didn't realize the others were staring at her until Cheryl bumped her arm. "Kerri?"

"I'm sorry, what?" Kerri wanted to hide. She really was an idiot.

"Don't worry about it." Eric pointed at the last three truffles. "You really should go into business. Those were excellent."

"I noticed you didn't try the peanut butter." Kerri tried to tease, but she was so tired her voiced didn't have any pep to it. It sounded a bit whiny.

"I was tempted, and that's saying a lot because I can't stand peanut butter." Eric looked all around the kitchen, and Kerri wondered what he was thinking. When his gaze found hers again, he looked startled. "I should go and let you get some sleep."

"We're so glad you came tonight." Cheryl led him down the hall to the living room; Kerri trailed behind. "Where should Kerri meet you for your tour of the town Wednesday?"

"Mom—" Her hands might feel cold, but her face was warm enough. "Stop trying to push him around. It's not like Eureka Springs is so large he can't figure it out on his own."

"Sweet pea?" Kerri's dad came out of the dining room. His voice held that same quality he used when he was disappointed in her. It made her feel ten years old again.

"Sorry, Daddy." Kerri knew she shouldn't snap at her mom.

"I'd love for you to show me around, but you don't have

to if you don't want to." Eric buttoned his coat. "I'm sure you've got better things to do."

Kerri loved his dimple when he smiled. She sighed. Showing him around town would be so much better than sitting at home all day feeling sorry for herself. Plus, she'd need a plan before she saw Jaya and Brynn at church. They would try and make plans for her day off if she wasn't prepared. After Mic's response to her problems she didn't think she could handle the other two. She'd made him *cry*.

The real question was, could she spend an entire day with Eric and not get attached to the yummy man? Of course she could. She just had to remember she wasn't dating material and he would leave eventually. Everything would be fine.

"I can show you around if you want." Kerri tried to make it sound like it was something she did every day. "How about I meet you in your hotel lobby at nine o'clock Wednesday morning?"

"Or I can come pick you up." His smile lit up the whole room.

"I guess that would be fine."

"Great. I'll be here at nine then." Eric tipped an imaginary hat at them. "Thank you so much for dinner and the wonderful company. I'll see you in a couple days."

Kerri stood in the doorway with her parents and watched Eric crawl through the passenger side of his car. He waved before backing out. A sinking loneliness settled on her as his taillights disappeared down the hill.

I'm in so much trouble.

6

ℰric towel dried his hair in preparation for meeting the realtor. They had only looked at two apartments the previous afternoon, and today he planned to look at houses for rent. He wanted to feel like a part of the community while maintaining some privacy. Perhaps he should think of going to church next week. Everyone around here seemed to go. That's why his realtor had only spent a few hours with him instead of all day. He had to admit, he had wondered which church Kerri went to more than once as the day passed.

He pulled on his pants and glanced at the lump of clay sitting on the table. After dinner with the Mannings, he'd pulled out the box of material and started working it into shape. He hadn't planned, simply let his fingers find their way to what was waiting to be revealed. There wasn't much to look at yet, but Eric had a good idea where it was headed. *I'll have to be extra careful not to get emotionally involved with this project.*

He shook his head. Isn't that why he left New York? He

needed to reconnect with his art on an emotional level. *The art, not the inspiration for it.*

His phone rang, interrupting his thoughts. A quick look at the screen revealed the caller.

"Hey Mom."

"Hi, I saw your picture in the paper with a tall blonde woman. Who is she?" Her voice sounded much too hopeful.

"You remember my agent." He shrugged his way into a t-shirt, then reached for a button up.

"That's right. You looked cozy with her. Do you like her?"

"It's just business. She likes the cameras more than she likes me." He cradled the phone to his ear and finished dressing.

"Oh. I worry about you being alone. There has to be some nice girls there in New York. Why are they so hard to find?"

"Mom, you don't have to worry about me. Anyway, I'm not in New York at the moment. I'm somewhere a lot nicer. Slower paced. I think you'd like it."

"Really? It's good to hear you're traveling. Is this for work or are you finally living a little?"

"Both. You were right at Christmas. I needed a break, take the time to find my inspiration again."

Eric heard his mother squeal on the other end of the line. "I'm so glad! Where did you go? The beach? Some hidden mountain hideaway?"

"I'm in Arkansas."

There was a pause, and it sounded like his mother knocked something over. "Arkansas? I don't understand. What's in Arkansas?"

"Peace and quiet. I found this quaint little town with a thriving artist community. I'm hoping to rent a house and see what happens."

"That's great! I wish you could have come home though. Patricia's niece is in town. You might have liked her."

"Mom." Eric shook his head and bent down in preparation for putting shoes on. "Stop trying to set me up."

"You're twenty-six. Don't you think it's time to find someone special to share your life with?"

He rolled his eyes, grateful she hadn't Skyped him. "Mom, I'm still young. There will be plenty of time for that later. Right now I need to concentrate on my art."

"Hmmpf. I saw the photos of your last pieces. They looked a little flashy to me. I didn't see any of you in them. You need something more in your life, something to wake you up again."

Eric sighed. "I know. That's why I'm here."

"Good. May I make a suggestion?"

"What?"

"Find a nice girl to settle down with."

Kerri's face popped into his mind. For a moment in the kitchen, he'd had visions of having dinner every day with her. He quickly shook his head in an effort to erase the thoughts. The last thing he needed was to start seeing her in that way.

"Mom, you're hopeless."

His mother laughed. "All I want is for you to give someone a chance."

"Been there, done that. If you recall it didn't work out for me."

"Sweetheart, I knew Vanessa was wrong for you from the beginning. Don't let her ruin the rest of your life."

"I've got to go, Mom." Eric sighed.

"Okay, just consider finding someone to kiss for Valentine's Day."

"Bye, Mom." He hung up, but couldn't help letting his

mom's words bounce around his head. It was lucky Vanessa had left him before their wedding. He was strings free if nothing else. Now, if only he could be callous enough to enjoy kissing someone without hoping for any kind of relationship.

One thing was for sure. For the next two days he would look at houses and avoid bead shops at all costs.

~

*A*fter several days of looking at houses with the realtor, Eric finally picked his place on Monday. Most of them were cute, and some had great lighting, but none of them felt right. Then they'd looked at a log cabin for sale with an extra building for his studio. It was less than a mile from Kerri's house on Spring Street. It would need some updates, but he liked the warmth of the wood floors and the way the trees hugged the back yard. He could envision his studio in the separate cottage. As for the house, all he could think about was how Kerri would fit there. How she would look standing by the counter while he tied the apron around her waist. It was a silly thought, but the house as a whole felt right because he could picture her there.

So much for not thinking about her as more than a model for his project. He needed to focus on something controllable. He told the realtor he'd think about it and made his way to Frank's shop. This time he studied each sculpture on display. They were mixed mediums, but they all hummed with life and motion.

"Eric, good to see you again." Frank joined him beside one of the larger pieces depicting a girl reaching out to a bird in flight. "That one is based on a girl I know named

Sarah. Technically she's a woman now, but in many ways she's still this little girl afraid to let go and find her wings."

"I can see it in her face. It's wonderful. Hope you don't mind me dropping in."

"Of course not. I love company while I work." Frank jerked his thumb toward the back room. "Come on back."

"Thanks." Eric followed, shifting the weight of the bag he carried. "I brought something to work on too. Is that all right?"

"Even better. I'm still chipping away at this block of wood. What will you be working on?" He picked up his tools and stared intently at the stump in front of him.

"I'm playing around with an idea. A study of expressions in clay." Eric set the pack down and pulled out a large lump wrapped in plastic bags and damp paper. "I started this Sunday and am ready to work on details."

"Let's see then." Frank left his wood to clear a spot on the workbench for Eric.

Eric unwrapped the bag. As he unfolded the paper, a head shaped oval revealed itself at half scale. Eyes, nose, and mouth had been roughed in. Frank took it in his hands, turning it one way and then the other.

"You've got a good start. Anyone I might know?"

"Maybe." Eric took it back, wondering why he suddenly felt uncomfortable. "Do you think she'd be upset? She has such an expressive face, I couldn't resist. Her bone structure is remarkable."

Frank laughed. "That it is. I don't think she'd mind, but be careful. Something's hurt my girl and I don't want you adding to it. Mind if I ask what your intentions are?"

"What do you mean? I just want to sculpt her."

"Uh huh. I may be old, but I'm not blind, or dead. I saw the way you two looked at each other. Heck, I could almost feel the sizzle in the air." Frank shook his finger at Eric. "Maybe you just haven't figured it out yet."

"Sure, I like her. She's nothing like any other girl I've ever met, but she's not interested, and I haven't found a place to rent. I'm not sure if I want to buy, so who knows how long I'll stay. The last thing I want is to complicate matters and hurt her."

"Good. Don't get me wrong, you seem like a nice guy, but Kerri is one of ours and she's sad enough right now." Frank wandered back to his wood.

"What happened? Why did she come home?" Eric sat down and started shifting bits of clay around, shaping cheek bones.

"Well now, that's Kerri's secret to keep or tell. All I can say is, I miss the carefree girl that used to sit in my shop for hours. Sometimes her friends would come with her, and I've never seen a livelier bunch. They keep me young. Now she seems lost. She deserves better than whatever she's dealing with."

"She didn't tell you either?" Eric almost smirked.

"Not yet. I figure she will when she's ready. I've never met a more caring girl than that one, but she's also a thinker. Gets her in trouble sometimes because she overthinks things when she should just follow her heart."

"I've only known her a few days and can see that." Eric closed his eyes and pictured Kerri sitting on the floor in this very room.

Her eyes had been round with surprise. She looked up with such innocence and something close to fear. He could tell by the way she shrunk down into her sweater that she wanted to disappear, but he still didn't know why. As he remembered the expression on her face, he let his fingers shape the clay. At times he used tools for detailing, and Kerri's face began to emerge from the material.

Eric and Frank both got lost in their various projects, and the hours flew by. Every once in a while, Frank left the room to visit with customers or a local that stopped in. Eric enjoyed the peace and the easy friendship he felt with the older man. He was glad Kerri had so many people who loved her and were determined to watch out for her. His decision to stay away from her for the last couple of days had been the right decision. She would be just fine without him.

"Let's see it now." Frank came back in and handed Eric a cup of coffee.

"Thanks." Eric took a sip and found the brew to be quite strong. Just what he needed after sitting for so long. "She's not finished but coming along. Something feels off. What do you think?" He held the head up for Frank to get a better view.

"Not bad. Not bad at all. You're right though. Could be she's bald."

Eric chuckled. "I'll work on that later. It's something else though. I can't quite put my finger on it."

"When was the last time you saw her?" Frank had a twinkle in his eye.

Eric set the sculpture down. "Friday night."

"So you haven't seen her for three days?"

"No sir."

"Why not?"

"It's not a good idea. We'll be spending all day Wednesday together, so I didn't want to bother her."

Frank laughed and slapped him on the shoulder. "You keep telling yourself that boy. We both know the truth. You already need her like the air you breathe and that scares the crap out of you."

"I wouldn't put it that way." Eric dampened some paper towels and carefully wrapped the head. Next he placed it inside the bag and put it all in his pack.

"You should 'cause it's the truth. Finish cleaning up and go see her. I bet you figure out what's off about your piece as soon as you do. Kerri's your muse."

Was she? Eric considered how he'd wanted to sculpt her that first day. It had been a long time since he'd felt such drive to create. Maybe she was his muse. He had to admit he'd been dying to see her, and that did scare him. Maybe he could catch a glimpse of her at work without entering the shop. That should be enough, right?

"I'll pass her shop on my way down the hill. I guess it wouldn't hurt to say hello." Eric picked up his pack and waved goodbye. "Thanks for letting me hang out today. I'll have to return the favor if I get my own place."

"I'd like that. Tell that pretty girl I said hello." Frank waved back with a big grin.

Eric shook his head as he left. How was it he always ran into matchmakers? At least this one wasn't sneaky about it, and he seemed to have misgivings too. What was hurting Kerri? *None of my business.*

Eric took his time walking down the street. He looked in the windows of several shops, enjoying the clutter and the people browsing the wares. When he reached Beads and Baubles, he paused to look through the dusty window. Although it clouded the scene slightly, he could see Kerri talking to a woman by a display of crafting tools.

A motion off to the side caught his attention. Cheryl was waving at him from the front counter.

Busted.

He opened the door and stepped inside the warm shop.

Kerri had knelt down to talk to a young girl he'd missed in the window. The girl held her mom's hand while Kerri spoke to her.

"What's your favorite color?" she asked.

Within seconds of entering the shop, he could already tell what was missing from his sculpture. Her inner light. It radiated around her, touching everything and everyone with its warmth. He nodded at Cheryl and watched Kerri interact with the mom and child. She treated them with such kindness, never talking down to the girl who looked to be six or seven years old. By the time they came to the register, both customers were all smiles.

"Hi." Kerri's eyes seemed to light up even more when she looked at him.

How would he ever portray that with cold, lifeless clumps of mud? "Hey, just passing by and thought I'd see if we were still on for Wednesday."

"Of course. How's the house shopping going?" She waved to the woman as she finished checking out and left the shop.

"Okay. There aren't many places to rent at the moment. It's giving me more time to work on a few new projects though."

"That's great. About the work, not the rentals." She chewed on her bottom lip. "Maybe something will come open?"

"Yeah, the realtor is hopeful, so I'll give it a bit longer before considering other options."

"Oh." Kerri picked at a thread on the sweater she was wearing. "That makes sense."

Eric wondered at Kerri's sudden quiet. Why did he care so much when she wasn't smiling? And why did it drive him crazy that he didn't know what she was thinking? He could clearly see her sudden discomfort, but he didn't know why she felt that way.

"Well, I guess I should let you get back to work." He took a step back.

"We're glad you stopped by." Cheryl was busy stringing beads behind the counter. "You'll have to join us for dinner again soon."

"Thanks. See you Wednesday." He nodded to both women and retreated to the street. Frank had been right. He needed to see Kerri, it would help him work, but it also left him feeling empty when she wasn't around. That was a dangerous combination, and he'd have to be extra careful.

~

*K*erri's body was extra sore, but her stretching routine had her moving almost normally after ten minutes. She pulled her collection of pills from the side drawer. There were three she took every day and another seven she only took once a week. Some helped with the inflammation, others general pain. One of them suppressed her immune system in the hopes it would stop attacking her joints. They were all expensive.

Life with Steven might have made a difference. If they'd been married, and he had a good job, insurance would have covered most of her bills. Would his life have changed much because of her?

Kerri turned the shower to hot and her thoughts moved to Eric. If she let him know how he affected her, would he run the way Steven had? She shook her head and forced herself to think about Sunday instead of Eric.

After church, she'd hung out with her friends. Brynn had dyed her brown hair platinum blonde. It took Kerri all day to get used to it. Brynn kept them enthralled with her stories of the music industry. She might not be a rock star, but she had stories of opera divas to curl anyone's toes. Jaya was as flawless as ever. Her beauty and milk chocolate complexion hid her devastatingly brilliant mind. She was taking the semester off to get ready for her wedding in March.

The girls had encouraged her to look Eric up online after Mic had spilled the beans about him. Kerri had avoided it since that first failed attempt. She wasn't sure why, but part of her wanted to get to know him, not the internet version of him. The others were curious, and even though they meant well, their plan had backfired.

Eric had a promising career in front of him. Getting attached to her would change his future, and not for the better. She'd have to steer clear of him. If one short night had branded his face on her brain and his smile on her heart, what would an entire day do to her? No matter what, she couldn't let herself fall for another man that didn't need her troubles.

Those worries had circled around since Sunday night. By the time she finished showering Tuesday morning, she had talked herself out of spending the next day with him. However, she didn't have his phone number. She'd have to tell him face to face when he showed up on her front porch.

"Ugh!"

"What's wrong, Kerri?" Her mom stopped by the door. It was rare she stayed home, but this morning Kerri's dad had gone in to open the shop.

"I can't go tomorrow. Help me think of an excuse."

Cheryl hugged her daughter. "Why can't you go?"

Kerri buried her face in her mom's shoulder. "He's too...I don't know, but I can't."

Her mom pushed away so she could look into her daughter's face. "Honey, he's just a tourist. You've helped your Uncle James show people around lots when you were younger. This isn't any different."

"It is different."

Her mom smiled. "Only if you want it to be. Do you?"

"Yes. No." Kerri shook her head. "It can't be."

"Why not? He's a nice guy. Your dad and I like him. Why not see where it could lead?"

"Because I can't. Don't you get it? I'm just a mess of pain and emotions. He doesn't need that."

"Oh, sweetheart." Cheryl pulled her back in for a hug. "You're so much more than that, and if he, or any other guy, can't see it, then you're better off without them."

"I just feel so empty. All the things I wanted are lost to me now. Love, a family."

"Nonsense. You can still have all those things, but you don't have to worry about them now."

"But I do. Remember what Dr. Dahler said? Depending on how fast it progresses, I could only have fifteen years of good mobility left. How will I take care of children once that's gone? And what if I can't have children at all? Who would want me then?"

"The right man will come along. We just have to leave it up to God." Cheryl smiled through her own tears. "Come on, chin up. We'll have breakfast, enjoy our day, and tomorrow will be a piece of cake. Just be yourself."

"It's too hard to be around him. He's someone I would have liked before all this happened."

"You agreed to take him around town. Do that much and if you don't want to see him after that, you don't have to."

"Okay." *I'll pretend he's Mic. We'll be two friends hanging out.* No matter what happened, she wouldn't let herself hope for more than that. Eric was a great guy. Easy to talk to, easy to look at. He made her laugh, and she needed more of that. Satisfied that was all she needed from him, Kerri nodded. "I can do this."

"You'd better get your assignments done for today and tomorrow. There's no need to be worried about them while you're playing tour guide."

"Sure. I'm going to call Uncle James too. Maybe he can go with us."

"Three's a crowd."

"Exactly."

7

*K*erri slept better than she had since coming home. After their slightly uncomfortable visit on Sunday, Jaya and Brynn had surprised her on Tuesday with a dinner invitation. The time went a lot smoother with just the three of them and no boys around. Jaya was the perfect image of a woman in love. Spending the evening watching her eyes light up every time she mentioned Aiden made Kerri wish for the same chance at love. She ached to feel as cherished as Jaya obviously did. Those hopes made preparing for a day with Eric even more confusing.

She stood in front of the closet wondering what to wear. The outfit needed to be warm, but most of those clothes weren't cute. Shaking her head, she reached for an old multi-colored sweater dress. Girls didn't try to dress cute for guys that were just friends. Especially guys they knew were moving on soon. No matter what, Eric wasn't the answer to her romantic dreams.

Kerri dressed and apprised herself in the mirror. The dress would be warm. She paired it with black leggings and her knee-high boots. Warm, practical, and maybe a little cute. She left her hair down in soft curls but glared at the reflection. "No makeup though."

The doorbell rang as she grabbed a warm muffin from the kitchen. She picked up a second one and made her way through the living room. After a deep breath, she opened the door. Eric looked wonderful in a soft slate-colored sweater.

His dimple tugged at her imagination as he grinned down at her and winked. "Good morning."

"Morning." Kerri pushed a muffin forward to keep from touching that dimple. Did friends wink at each other? "Would you like a muffin?"

"Thanks." His fingers brushed hers as he took it from her.

Little spurts of energy sizzled up Kerri's arms, settling around her heart. She swallowed and stepped back to let him in.

Cheryl breezed into the living room. "Morning, Eric. Good to see you found us again."

"Good morning, Mrs. Manning." Eric dipped his head in her direction.

Cheryl smiled and disappeared into the kitchen. Kerri found she wasn't very hungry after all. She stood there holding her muffin and wondering how in the world she could survive an entire day with this man and escape with her heart. Maybe, just maybe she should give it a chance?

Eric ate his muffin in two bites. "Mmm, that was really good, thanks."

Kerri handed him the other one in her hand. "You ready for this?"

"Been looking forward to it all night." Eric ducked his

head a moment then looked back up. "I mean, how lucky am I to get a tour of town from a local?"

"Very!" Cheryl came back with her purse in hand. "Kerri used to help her uncle give tours in the summer."

"Mom, I didn't do much. However," Kerri turned to Eric, "I'm glad you dressed warm. I convinced my Uncle James to take us on the historic tram tour. He'll have to take us in the ranger though."

"Ranger?" Eric's brow shot up.

Kerri laughed. "Yes, I call it his souped up golf cart. It's a four-seat ATV. You can see the houses better that way than in a car. Plus the roads get pretty narrow in spots."

"Will you be okay?" His concern was evident in his voice.

"It's supposed to be in the mid-forties. I'll be fine." Kerri hoped her face wasn't showing how warm she felt at the moment. Steven had never worried about her comfort. It probably never entered his head he should even think of it.

Cheryl opened the closet door and pulled out Kerri's coat. "Well, off with the two of you. Kerri can show you pretty much everything in a few hours. Feel free to join us for dinner again. No point in wasting money at restaurants when we've got plenty."

"Thanks, Mrs. Manning."

"Please, call me Cheryl." She handed the coat to her daughter.

Just the sight of it and the five buttons made Kerri sigh. She took it and felt disappointed she was able to button it on her own. A quick glance at Eric showed his lips turned down and a little crease between his brows. Could it be he had hoped to button them for her?

"Come on then. What would you like to see first?" Kerri brushed past him and stepped onto the porch before he could see her grin like crazy.

"Could we just walk around town?" Eric followed close behind. "I'm still trying to get a feel for everything."

"Sounds good to me." Kerri noticed he had parked at the end of her drive, blocking both cars in. "I see you found a solution to your problem."

Eric opened her door. "A gentleman always finds a way."

Once he was settled in the driver's side, Kerri let him drive back to his hotel parking space. It didn't take them long. Traffic wasn't bad yet, but Kerri knew the cars and foot traffic would double in the next hour. The Grand Central lot might not be the best place to start the tour, but Main Street was close to all the shops on Spring Street. She refused to think of the stairs or the uphill climb. It would be worth it, right?

"Stay put." Eric pointed in her direction, making her laugh.

No one had ever made such a big deal out of opening the door for her. She kind of liked that he was as old fashioned as she was about some things. Eric reached down to help her out of the car. Kerri took his hand and stood before she realized how close that would put them. She could smell soap and aftershave. It sent a tingle straight to the flutters in her stomach.

"This is going to be one amazing day." His dimple kicked the jitters up a notch.

Kerri nodded. She found it hard to breathe. Or talk. Or think. Those abilities didn't return until he took a step away from her and dropped her hand. *Mercy.*

"Lead the way, Ms. Tour Guide."

You can do this. Just don't look at him too much. Focus on the town. Kerri took a deep breath. "Okay, let's walk that way. There are some stairs we can take to cut the corner."

"The ones from the other night?"

"Yes. We can walk up one side of the street and then back down the other to the trolley station. It will drive us all around the other parts of town, but we can do Downtown in about an hour."

"You've really thought this out." Eric placed his hand on the small of her back.

All Kerri's resolve not to look at him melted. She glanced up and wondered where he'd come from. Steven had never opened the door for her, had rarely felt the need to keep physical contact, and he'd never made her feel so alive without doing a darn thing.

"What?" His brow quirked upward.

"Nothing." Her cheeks flamed up again. "I'm just not used to gentlemen I guess."

They walked quickly, and soon Kerri really was warm all over. It felt glorious to not be cold. The wind wasn't blowing her away, and the exercise felt good. That good feeling dwindled a bit after the flight of old, uneven, narrow steps. A small hitch wormed its way into one hip. She pushed forward and hoped for a chance to stretch before it started hurting too much. Eric stayed close, but she made sure she was in front or behind him, so as to avoid unnecessary eye contact. The narrow sidewalks and other tourists made it easy.

Kerri showed him several of her favorite shops and introduced him to the owners. They were all like family to her. She loved how easily Eric fell into conversation with them. It's like he had the gift of making someone feel important. That had to be the reason she liked him so much.

I have to keep in mind I'm just like all these other people to him. After her little pep talk to herself, Kerri relaxed and let herself enjoy the morning, but she continued to avoid looking directly at his beautiful face.

"They have a blessing bowl in that one. I don't know the owners personally, they're fairly new, but I thought it was a sweet idea." Kerri pointed to another shop as they wandered down the hill back to the trolley station.

Eric paused by the window. "What's a blessing bowl?"

"We can go in if you want." Kerri suddenly needed to see what he thought about the bowl. Steven had made fun of it. Called it hokey and tree-huggerish.

They approached a table set against the back wall. It was covered with little knick-knacks that circled a large bowl. Kerri wasn't sure if it was stone or just painted pottery that looked like stone. Eric bent down to read the handwritten sign hanging above it.

"When the power of love replaces the love of power, then the world will know peace. Jimi Hendrix." He continued to read the rest about putting positive thoughts to lift the energy of the world silently. "Huh. That's pretty cool. Have you ever put something in the bowl?"

"Once." She shrugged. Did he really think it was cool?

"Maybe you should think of something to put in today. It says it will go out into the world as well as come back to you. In fact, I think I'll add something as well. I could use a little good luck."

"Really? What do you need luck for?" Kerri watched him grab a piece of paper from the little box by the bowl.

"Let's just say my art could use some help. My agent is waiting for a new collection."

"You have an agent? You must be pretty good." For some reason she didn't want him to know she'd looked him up. It felt too desperate.

"Maybe. I used to be. Nothing's really grabbed my attention in a while. I've just been doing commission pieces and they're okay, I guess." He wrote on the paper, folded it, and put it in the bowl.

"What did you write?" She tried to catch a glimpse of his paper.

"Nothing profound. Just 'Have the courage to chase your dreams.'"

Kerri sucked in a breath. What was her dream? It used to be the chocolate shop, but the idea didn't get her as excited as it used to. She didn't think it was just because of the RA either.

"What?" Eric touched her elbow briefly before pulling back. "Did I say something wrong?"

"No." Kerri shook her head and smiled the first real smile of the day. "No. You said exactly what I needed to hear."

"Oh?" His brow did that cute little lift thing it did when he had a question.

"Yeah, but do you think it's possible for dreams to change? I used to know what I wanted to do, now I'm not so sure."

"Sure, dreams change all the time. What did you used to want?"

"Just the chocolate shop my mom told you about. Jen and I kind of let it slip away, but she asked me to enter us in the Valentine's Chocolate Festival. I haven't done it, but I'm not sure why."

"Why wouldn't you? Even if it isn't where your passion lies, it could be fun and get the creative juices flowing again." Eric handed her a piece of paper. "Put a positive thought in the bowl and go for it."

Kerri took the pen. "Okay, here goes nothing." She scribbled a quick thought and tossed it in the bowl. "There. Now let's get to the trolley."

They headed outside. Kerri was glad the sun was shining and the wind was almost non-existent.

"So, what did you write?" Eric asked.

"Um, it isn't important."

"Sure it is. I told you mine." He touched her arm again.

"Okay. 'Every day is a second chance.' It's kind of like when Anne said, 'tomorrow is a new day with no mistakes in it.'"

"Anne?"

"From Anne of Green Gables."

"Oh I see." He'd been walking behind Kerri on the narrow sidewalk, but he stepped up beside her. "Every day is a second chance. I like it."

~

*E*ric enjoyed the walk with Kerri. She had been easy to talk to, and he loved the way she lit up around the people she loved. He almost didn't want to get on the trolley, but he figured riding would be warmer for her. She had avoided looking at him most of the morning and managed to stay a few steps ahead of him. As soon as the sidewalk widened, he moved up beside her but fought the urge to grab her hand.

"Is that the station over there?" He pointed to a small square-ish building with a trolley pulling up beside it.

"Yep. We can get passes and catch the next one." She glanced at him, but he noticed her gaze hit about shoulder level.

It puzzled him. He was used to women fawning all over him. Maybe he'd misread her interest at dinner the week before.

Eric moved to open the door but it opened automatically. Feeling a little silly he followed Kerri inside. At the desk she asked for two day passes.

"That'll be twelve dollars." The lady behind the desk was older. Maybe in her late fifties or early sixties. She looked bored out of her head.

Eric pulled out his wallet and paid for both tickets.

"I could have paid for mine." Kerri finally looked him in the face.

Her brown eyes were darker inside. Right now there was a little crease on her forehead like she was trying to figure something out. Eric reached out to smooth the line away like he could in the clay. She gasped in surprise at his touch, but she didn't pull away.

"You had—" Eric stopped short of telling her she had a wrinkle. He traced the side of her face, entranced with her delicate bone structure. As his mind processed how to incorporate the sensory input in the sculptures, he realized she was still staring at him. He let his hand fall away from her face. "Sorry."

"For what?" her voice sounded a little breathy.

"I didn't want to scare you."

"Why would you think this would scare me?"

"Well, you've avoided eye contact most of the morning." Eric watched her closely; loving once again how each emotion could clearly be read on her face. He had watched her interact with the other shop owners. It was easy to see the love she had for them, as well as the joy at seeing them again. There were also moments of embarrassment when they asked why she was home from school. She handled those questions with grace, not delving into her problems or complaining. Now her eyes showed something that looked like regret.

"I'm sorry. It's just—" Her cheeks and neck turned a pretty shade of pink.

"The blue route trolley just pulled in. It's the last one for half an hour, so you don't want to miss it," the lady pointed to the doors on the right.

"Thank you." Eric put his hand on Kerri's back and guided her out the door. He wondered what she would have said if she'd not been interrupted, but he didn't push it. "Is the blue line what we want?"

"It is. Uncle James will cover the red route with us later."

There were only three other people on the trolley. Kerri sat behind one of the wheel hubs, and Eric joined her. Heat from the vent blew on their feet. She sighed and stretched her legs towards it, making Eric more willing to put up with the stuffy air.

Kerri pointed out different buildings as they drove: a Victorian hotel that had been moved to Eureka Springs from its original location, various shops and places she'd hung out with her friends growing up. No one else got on the trolley at either of the other two mandatory stops.

"Is it always so quiet?" Eric looked at the different styles of hotels they passed.

"By the weekend things will pick up for the Mardi Gras activities. It won't slow down again until after Valentine's. We'll get one more lull before the new season starts."

"You celebrate Mardi Gras here?"

"Yep. It gets a bit crazy. I've missed the last few years, and before that I sort of hid at home. It's not really my kind of scene." She turned back to the window.

"Why isn't it your thing?"

"I'm not really the partying kind. The only part that sounds fun is the ball at the Crescent Hotel. I've never been though." She shrugged.

"Why not?"

Kerri rubbed her arm. "It's silly."

Eric reached out and took her hand in his. He massaged her palm and wrist, working his way up her forearm the way he'd seen her father do.

"What are you doing?" her eyes widened.

"Do your arms hurt?" He continued to knead the tight muscles in her arm, marveling at how smooth her skin was.

"A little, but this isn't necessary." She tugged a bit, but he held on.

"Is it helping?" Slowly he worked his way back to her hands, where he rubbed in circular motions. He could feel the tension sliding away as he caressed each finger. Eric almost laughed at the expression on her face. Sheer terror and a bit of something else. He could see the blush rising again. Good, because he had felt the need to touch her all day and this felt safe.

"It...I..." She swallowed and looked over his shoulder. "Maybe."

Eric chuckled. "Now are you going to answer my question?"

"Which one?"

"Why you never went to the ball?"

"I don't know. Maybe it's the noise and couples all over each other." Her free hand drifted to her hair where she proceeded to curl a lock of hair around and around.

Eric fought the urge to touch that perfectly formed curl. "Is it because you didn't have a boyfriend?"

"I've had lots of boyfriends." She turned her nose up in the air, making her curls bounce on her shoulders.

"I bet you have." The thought of another man kissing her sobered him. It jabbed at a spot right behind his eyes. He switched to her other arm. *Stop. She deserves to be loved.*

Eric took a deep breath as the bus pulled back into the station where they'd boarded. "That didn't take long."

"No, it's longer in the summer." Kerri didn't make a move to get off. "Everything is just a bit prettier once the leaves come in. There's more to do at the lakes, caves, and other places to hike."

"Do you like that kind of stuff?" He sat still. If she didn't want to get off, he wouldn't either.

"I love being outside. Always have." The little furrow appeared on her forehead again. "I'll miss those things the most."

"What do you mean?"

8

"Oh, I didn't mean anything." Kerri pushed her hair behind her ear. She almost slipped and told him about the RA. A quick glance at her watched showed it was almost 11:30. Perfect timing. "If we stay on, we can ride the trolley to the visitor's center to meet my uncle. He'll drive us around some of the historic homes and to the Crescent Hotel. That's one stop most people don't want to miss."

"Kerri? You mentioned doctor visits that first day we met. It's obvious you're in pain sometimes. What's wrong?" Eric stopped massaging her arm.

His gravity pulled her in as he placed both hands on the back of her elbows. Those little spots of warmth were a direct contrast to her cold fingers. The cool air rushed in as people exited the trolley, and a shiver traveled down her back. Time slowed. Kerri gazed into Eric's eyes and wished she had the nerve to tell him everything. Would he understand? *Of course not. He'll run like Steven*.

"I...I don't want to talk about it, okay? It doesn't matter anyway." Kerri backed away, determined to keep from falling farther into his embrace.

Eric sighed but nodded his head. "I'm sorry for asking."

"No, it's fine. Eventually I'll have to tell everyone. If you stick around, you'll know all about it. Secrets don't keep in little places like this. It's just that you make me feel normal, and I like that. When we're together I can pretend I'm healthy. I want to enjoy that for today." Kerri's throat clogged. She swallowed the thickness that signaled the oncoming tears. "Please, let's just forget it."

"Of course." Eric's voice was gentle.

He reached for her hand and gave it a squeeze. She was surprised when he didn't let it go. It was another sweet moment where he took care of her without making her feel weak. Kerri blinked away the moisture that blurred her vision. She allowed herself to take strength from the strong hand holding hers. *Is this how Jaya feels with Aiden?*

Kerri shivered again. "Sorry, guess I got a chill."

Eric wrapped an arm around her and tucked her to his side where she fit perfectly. Kerri knew she shouldn't stay so close to him. However, she couldn't bring herself to move away. Nothing could ever come from this friendship, but was it so wrong to pretend for one five minute drive that she could have what her friend did?

Kerri tried not to obsess over it. The warm body next to hers made it nearly impossible. She wondered what he was thinking about. What did he feel for her? How would he react when he learned about her RA? What if he didn't run?

It doesn't matter. He wouldn't stay forever. His life was waiting for him out there. For all she knew, he had a girl-friend somewhere. A sinking feeling pressed her deeper into the seat.

Eric peered down at her. "What has you so pensive?"

"Um, nothing important."

"You sure?"

"Yep. We're here." Kerri pointed out the window. She could see her uncle parked in the first spot. His dark green ranger sported golden *fleur de lis*, brightly-colored Mardi Gras masks, and battery operated lights. He often used it as a mini float in the parade. "That spot of color is my uncle."

"Wow, he didn't do that for me did he?"

Kerri laughed. "No, he must have decided to ride in the parade this year. Come on."

They stepped off the trolley.

"Kerri-berri! It's good to have you home. Will you be staying the summer? I could use you on the route." The tall, robust man pulled her into a bear hug.

"Maybe. Uncle James, this is Eric Hunt."

"Nice to meet you." James extended his hand to the younger man. "Hope you're ready for some history. We've got lots of it to share."

"I really appreciate you taking me around." Eric nodded toward the ATV. "That's some chariot you've got here."

James laughed and led them to the four-seater cart. "Well, it'll get the job done anyway. Hop in and we'll get started."

A thick blanket sat in the back seat. Kerri picked it up and hugged it to herself. "Did Mom call you?"

Her uncle smiled. "She sure did. Said this friend of yours was worried you'd be too cold without one."

Kerri turned in time to see Eric blush.

"You thought of this?" she asked him.

"You weren't supposed to know." He shrugged.

"Well, the least I can do is share it with you. Come on."

Kerri slid onto the back seat and unfolded the blanket. Eric sat beside her. They tucked the blanket around their legs and James pulled out of the parking lot.

∽

*E*ric enjoyed listening to James talk about the various houses and town's history. He liked snuggling up to Kerri even more. The more she tried to pull away, the more he felt like chasing her. Surely, if she were like the other women he knew she'd have given in by now and returned his flirting efforts.

"Did you know we have over eighty miles of stone retaining walls here?" James glanced over his shoulder for half a second before turning back to the road. "We have a saying. If you want to keep it, you wall it!"

Eric laughed along with him. *Maybe that's what I need, a wall—all around sweet Kerri. Then I'd always be able to find my little muse.*

However, she stared straight ahead, avoiding his gaze again. She didn't exactly give him the cold shoulder, but she wasn't burrowing into his embrace like he wanted. In fact, she had that haunted look again. Maybe she *was* afraid of him? He gave her some space as they pulled up to the Crescent Hotel.

Even with the trees bare, and the garden in hibernation mode, the grounds of the Crescent Hotel were nice. Eric could only imagine what they'd look like in the spring. The hotel itself was a sight to behold. The white stone gave a sense of solid history.

James parked the ATV under the awning by the entrance. "Here we are. Why don't you two walk the grounds and then check out the observation deck? I'm going to sit in the lobby and chat with friends. Let me know when you're ready to head out."

"Thanks, we'll take our time." Kerri rolled the blanket

up and left it on the seat. She finally turned her gaze to Eric "Where do you want to go first?"

"Do you need to warm up?" Eric took the moment to really check her out. Her cheeks had a nice rosy glow, but her lips were a tad bit on the blue-ish side. What if he warmed them up for her?

"I'm fine." She turned away before he could act on the impulse. "Let's do a quick circuit outside and then take our time inside."

"Lead the way." He liked following her and the view it provided. Perhaps he'd have to think about some full body sculptures. His phone buzzed in his pocket. "Just a minute."

"No problem." She paused on the path and studied the gazebo that was attached to the hotel by some kind of patio.

Eric glanced at the text from his Realtor asking about the house. He'd thought about it a lot over the last couple of days as he'd lived and tried to work in the hotel room. Eureka Springs had a nice feel to it. Even if he didn't stay, he would like to visit. Perhaps bring his mom or sisters. They'd eat this place up. Eric watched Kerri as she touched a branch of a bush. All the crazy thoughts about staying here, with her, zipped through his mind.

It's an investment, nothing else. Eric tapped out a quick message.

Why not? Let's do it.

He paused half a second before hitting send. Was buying a house the right thing to do? He knew he didn't want to return to New York City, but could he buy a home here? Home. A rush of relief brought the smile back to his face. He'd put his loft up for sale and have plenty of money to buy the house and another one in North Carolina if he wanted. He hit send.

Eric jogged across the lawn to join Kerri by a fountain.

She leaned against the side, facing the hotel. "Sorry about that. I'm ready now."

"No problem. Everything okay?"

"Yep. I bet this is pretty when the fountain is on and the grass is all green." He reached out to touch the cold stone wall.

"This is one of the favorite wedding spots." She pointed to the building. "They like having the hotel in the background. Did you know this is made from local limestone?"

"Nice." He found that the hotel couldn't keep his attention with her standing beside him. "Beautiful."

"Come on." Kerri headed back to the path by the gazebo. "The other side was the original front entrance." She led him past spa windows. It looked empty for the moment. She paused at a massive hot tub and pointed down the hill. "We should go down there to get the full effect."

"Sounds good. I've noticed there are steps everywhere. Between the buildings on the strip, leading up to houses, here. Is this how you stay in such good shape?"

She brushed her fingers through her hair and sort of shook her head. "I guess it doesn't hurt." Then she laughed. "My friend Jen used to make me going running with her three times a week. I hated it, but it was good for me."

"Very good." They reached the bottom of the stairs, and Eric pulled his gaze away from her shapely legs to stare at the tall trees on the hillside and up to the front porch. "You're right, this is amazing."

"I love looking at the old photos of it. Come on, I'll show you inside." She was moving again, as if she couldn't stand still.

She was halfway up the steps before he caught up with her. He noticed that she took each step a little slower than the last one, and she'd paled a little.

"Are we in a hurry?" He worried about the little lines that had reappeared between her eyes.

Kerry pulled in a deep breath. "No, sorry. I just wanted to get the stairs out of the way."

He watched her try to discreetly rub at her hip. Had the stairs caused her more pain? They walked to a circular courtyard of sorts in front of the stairs leading up to the doors.

"Kerri!" Two women jumped up from a set of rockers on the porch.

One was blonde, very well dressed, and beaming down at them. Her friend had an exotic look with her mocha skin and dark eyes. The blonde one dragged the other woman down the steps.

"Slow down, I don't want to break an ankle before my wedding!" The darker woman laughed but kept pace with her friend.

"Sorry, Jaya." The blonde woman stopped in front of them. She pulled Kerri into a hug. "Is this why you couldn't spend the day with us?"

Kerri twisted her hands. Eric watched her take a deep breath and let it go before pasting a smile on her face. It didn't look fake, but it was cautious. Like she couldn't decide if she was happy to see them or not.

Interesting.

"Yeah, I told you I was going to show Eric around town." Kerri hugged Jaya as well.

"This the guy you were telling us about?" The blonde one took her time looking him over.

"Eric, this is Brynn and Jaya. Two of my friends from high school." She pointed to them, confirming their names.

Eric liked knowing she'd been talking about him with

her friends, and the way she blushed when her friend brought it up. *Wonder what she told them*?

"Nice to meet you Eric." Jaya held out her hand.

"You too."

"What are you guys doing here?" Kerri asked.

"Jaya needed to get reacquainted with the hotel grounds. You know, decide where the best spot for her wedding will be." Brynn spoke to Kerri but moved in to shake Eric's hand. "But never mind about that."

Eric shook it, but the woman didn't let go right away. She clasped the hand with both of hers and stepped closer. Everything about her reminded Eric of the women he'd left in the city.

"You're the sculptor we looked up Sunday afternoon." Brynn moved smoothly from standing in front of him to standing arm in arm with him. She placed herself between Eric and Kerri, then continued to talk, leaving no time for a response. "Last fall I saw one of your exhibits. It was the one on nature and fantasy. It was amazing."

"You didn't mention that on Sunday." Kerri looked back and forth between her friends. It was clear she was confused about something.

"You kept trying to change the subject, so what was the point?" Brynn pursed her lips and turned back to Eric. "Have you seen the inside yet?"

Kerri had mentioned him to her friends but didn't want to talk about him? And why hadn't she admitted that she had looked him up online?

"We were just heading that way." Eric tried to get a look at Kerri's face, but she had turned to Jaya. When she finally faced him again, her smile appeared forced. With the fake blonde oozing attention on him, he recognized once again how genuine Kerri had always been around him. She didn't try this hard to get his attention and yet she had it, even when she wasn't with him.

"Eric? Hello, where did you run off too? I bet you're dreaming up some new art. I've always loved the artistic types. I'm a singer myself. I know exactly what it's like to get lost in your work." Brynn smiled, talked, and dragged him toward the hotel.

"It's true. I'm almost always thinking about my projects. You sing?" He looked up the multitude of steps and wondered if Kerri could handle more.

"Singing is everything!" Brynn was definitely enthusiastic.

Kerri and her friend Jaya dropped behind them. He barely heard Kerri's sigh over Brynn's constant chatter as they started up the stairs. She was saying something about the hotel being haunted, but it didn't interest him. All he could think about was Kerri wearing herself out on the steps. He turned back to see Kerri and Jaya arm in arm working their way up.

"How much have you walked today?" Jaya asked, barely loud enough for him to hear.

Kerri didn't answer but shook her head. She caught him staring and quickly looked away. Brynn tugged on his arm, preventing him from going down to help Kerri.

"Jaya's always planned to get married here." Brynn waved at the hotel with a flourish. "She'll be a beautiful bride."

Jaya blushed. "As long as Aiden's waiting for me under the arbor I don't really care about anything else."

Kerri hugged Jaya again. "I can't believe you two are finally getting married."

Eric enjoyed watching the women interact. Kerri had

relaxed some, even though it looked like she might be leaning on Jaya. He caught her shiver.

"Ladies, why don't we move indoors? I'm afraid I've kept Kerri outside too long. My guess is you'd all like a chance to warm up." He opened the door and held it while they walked in.

"You do look tired, Kerri. Are you all right?" Brynn asked as they entered the lobby.

Eric listened closely to Kerri's answer while looking at the deep wood trim in the lobby. A large fireplace filled one corner of the foyer.

"I'm fine, thanks though." Kerri didn't look fine though. She looked like she might collapse any moment.

"It was really nice to meet you, but I think I should find Kerri's uncle and get her home." Eric managed to get his arm free from Brynn.

"You too. You know," Brynn leaned closer. "If you get bored while you're here, you can always give me a call. I'd love to show you some of the night life around here."

"Brynn," Kerri's face was flushed. "Won't you be busy planning the bridal shower?"

"Jaya isn't hard to plan for." Brynn finally moved to stand by her friend. "I can do both."

"Brynn, I don't think that's what she means." Jaya nudged her.

Eric took the opportunity to slide next to Kerri and take her hand. "Thanks for the offer Brynn, but Kerri is taking great care of me." He noticed Brynn's eyes grow round with surprise for half a second before she covered it up with a pageant smile.

She clasped her hands together and beamed at them. "I'm so sorry, I didn't realize. Kerri, you were holding out on us."

Kerri squirmed beside him. Her gaze darted to him, then back to her friends. The whole time she tried to pull her hand free, but he held on. "We're not...he's not. I mean, we just met and well, you know."

"Oh! That thing you told us about?" Brynn waved her hands dismissively in the air. "I think you're being silly. It can't be as bad as you think."

Kerri's eyes widened as she sent a panicked look at Jaya.

Brynn missed it. "But don't you see? If it works out, you don't have to go through this alone. And how lucky are you to have caught an artist that actually makes money. "

"What?" Eric jerked around to look at Kerri. Her expressive face didn't do her any favors. She was clearly mortified.

"Brynn, too soon." Jaya hissed while shaking her head. "They've only known each other a week."

Kerri turned even paler. "We've got to go."

Eric dropped her hand. Do what alone? Pay for medical expenses? He knew she was sick, but he still didn't know what that entailed. Did she need financial help? She hadn't denied he could pay for medical bills. He scrambled to follow her across the room to her uncle, who happened to be enjoying an ice cream cone. Eric barely registered the ice cream shop in the lobby.

"Kerri?" He didn't catch her before she reached James.

"Sorry we took so long." Kerri glanced over her shoulder at the two women. "We can go now."

"Okay, Kerri-berri." James didn't act the least surprised it had only been ten minutes or so since they'd arrived and hauled himself out of the chair.

"Kerri, we need to talk." Eric touched her elbow as she followed James out the door. Eric's thoughts were spinning.

"I promise there isn't any reason Brynn should jump to conclusions like she did," Kerri said.

He wanted to believe her, but she sounded so defeated. Was that because she had planned on using him to get whatever she needed to be healthy? His heart sank. Of course she had. How could he have been fooled into thinking she didn't want anything from him? She was just better at the game than all those women who came before. He tried to relax his hands that had fisted by his side. How had he forgotten in such a short time how manipulative women could be?

When they were safely in the ATV and on their way, she turned to him. "Please, let me explain."

"It's fine. Really." Eric studied her face. There had to be some kind of sign to show what she really felt. She was so close he could see tiny pale freckles along her nose and cheeks. Her eyes had that slight deer in the headlights look to them. How could she look so innocent? "It's getting kind of late. Maybe we should head back?"

Kerri blinked. She took a deep breath and looked at the back of her uncle's head. "Sure. We can finish the tour some other time if you want."

James kept quiet up front. He continued driving as if he couldn't hear a thing going on behind him. Eric felt a little flustered all the same. Part of him wanted to walk away and forget everything, another part wanted to confront her about Brynn's assumption. There had to be more to this story, she didn't seem the type to make things up. No matter what, he couldn't do it with her uncle sitting right there. It made everything extra awkward.

"I know you're busy." He almost whispered. "Don't worry about the rest of the tour."

James interjected from the front. "How about we visit the Christ of the Ozarks and then call it a day. It won't take but twenty more minutes and I'll get you back to your hotel."

Eric rolled his neck to ease some of the growing tension. Was this a family conspiracy? Cheryl had definitely been pushing for him to get together with Kerri. Every part of him wanted to flee somewhere he could be alone and think, but his parents hadn't raised him to be rude. Maybe James wasn't part of the plan to trap Eric into taking care of someone's medical bills. Even if he was, twenty minutes wouldn't kill him now that he was on his guard.

"That's fine."

≈

erri felt the change as soon as the words left Brynn's mouth. Eric's hand had tightened before he dropped hers. Then he'd moved away ever so slightly. He'd been right there all morning. Standing close enough she couldn't escape that warmth or his wonderful smell. Now, both were gone. She'd avoided his gaze all day even though she could feel it hot on her face. Now, he wouldn't look her in the eye.

Even his voice had lost its warmth.

They sat in silence as James drove them to the giant Christus. Brynn was so clueless! Sure, Kerri hadn't admitted to her friends how much she liked Eric, but she thought it had been clear. Wasn't that why they had pushed so hard for her to look him up? And yet, Brynn flirted and then babbled on about Kerri's problems. Had Eric turned cold because Brynn reminded him Kerri was sick? Or did it have something to do with money?

She needed something to think about other than the fact Eric no longer sat so close that their legs touched. She had been nice and warm on the earlier ride. Now the cold that seeped around her wasn't just on the outside. "Uncle James, why don't you tell Eric about the statue?"

"You mean our milk carton with arms?" James laughed and laughed. "Kerri says you're a sculptor?"

"Yes sir." Eric didn't laugh the way most people did when they heard the local nickname for the statue.

"Wait until you see it. You'll have to walk the short trail to take it in up close."

"Of course. How close are we?" Eric asked in that same detached voice.

It hurt in a way Kerri hadn't expected. She missed his warm teasing. It proved she'd been right about not spending too much time with him. Brynn had broken the spell. Whether it was her sickness or the fact she would need help, his true colors were coming out. The saddest part was she had decided to give him a chance.

"We're almost there. The turn is coming up." Kerri tried to speak normally. This was what she wanted, right?

Eric didn't respond. James took the turn faster than he should and it thrust Kerri into Eric's side. He held onto the roof with one hand to keep from falling out and held Kerri with his other arm. As soon as they straightened out, he let go and shimmied closer to the edge of the seat. The brief contact only confirmed what she had lost at the hotel.

"Oops." James piped up.

"What's up with the crazy driving?" Kerri grumbled.

"Just excited I guess. I'll park right next to the sidewalk. Kerri do you want to show him the amphitheater too?"

"Um, maybe not today," Kerri murmured.

"Okay." James threw on the brakes and parked.

"Seriously? You're going to give us whiplash." Kerri shoved the blanket off her legs and hopped out her side of the ATV. "Come on, let's get this over with."

Eric shot her a funny look, but she didn't care. He was the one that turned cranky first. To make matters worse, her hips and knees had been screaming at her for the last hour. She needed to get home and take her medicine.

They walked in silence, and Kerri tried to calm down. Maybe she should just ask him what he was so agitated about? If it was her illness, she would understand. If it was money related she could assure him that wasn't her intention. She'd never been good about confronting people, but she took another deep breath and decided she didn't have anything to lose.

"You wanted to talk?" she kept her gaze forward. "Now would be a good time to clear this up."

"I told you it's fine. I'm not upset." His voice didn't match the words.

"Then why are you acting like—"

He cut her off. "Let's not talk about it. We'll look at the statue and then I'll get you back to the shop."

Anger flared. *Seriously? Now he won't talk at all?* A new thought crept under her skin. What if he'd really been interested in Brynn? *Figures.*

Kerri put her frustration into motion, fairly stomping down the sidewalk a few steps before stopping to stand in Eric's path. "No, this is stupid. Why are you so upset? I didn't do anything wrong, and neither did my friends. And yet suddenly you're all cold and distant."

"I don't have a problem with your friends. It's you I have a problem with." He glared at her with his arms crossed over his chest.

He did like Brynn.

"Of course it's me." Kerri's body hummed with pain and anger. She feared it might be the only thing keeping her standing. It bubbled out in a mumble. "No one's as perfect or blonde as Brynn."

"What did you say? If you need to say it, say it loud enough I can hear."

"It doesn't matter. I don't have all day."

"That's nice. Love the attitude. You've been hiding that pretty well the last few days." He stepped around her and continued down the trail.

"At least I didn't pretend to be this wonderful gentleman before turning into a jerk."

"I'm the jerk? You're worse than Vanessa. At least she was honest about the fact she used me."

"Who's Vanessa?" Kerri had to jog to keep up with his longer strides.

"My ex-fiancée."

"You were engaged?"

"She left a week before our wedding because she found someone else to advance her career faster than I could. If she taught me anything, it's that women like you will always need more than I can give. I'm sick of people who only want my money or the publicity I can give them."

She tripped over her own feet when her legs almost gave out. Her body was not going to forgive her for the strain of the day.

"Don't even try the helpless routine." His voice was almost a sneer.

"What?" Kerri's thoughts were jumbled. Helpless? Engaged. He's sure I'm using him. She left him?

"I'm on to you, so stop pretending you need my help to walk in a straight line."

Kerri felt like throwing up. "I don't need anything from you. Not even your friendship. I'm so glad we didn't try for more. If you compare your friends to gold digging ex-fiancées, how do you treat your girlfriends?"

"You're just like them." He spat, the anger hardening his eyes.

He'd never believe her. He was running away from her as fast as he could, using any excuse.

"And you're just like Steven. Something turns out harder than you expected so you run away. Well, you can stop now." She pointed to the giant statue of Christ. "Feel free to walk around, do whatever sculptors do when comparing them-selves to others. Tell yourself whatever you need to in order to feel better about yourself. I'm going back to the cart." With that she spun and practically ran back to the parking lot.

Her heart ached at the loss. In spite of herself, she had hoped for at least the friendship he'd offered. She should have known better. No one is that perfect. He was just as emotionally scarred as she was, and neither of them could let the other in. Not really. Not now, probably not ever.

She tried to push her own disappointment to the side. He didn't trust her. Even though she understood, it still crushed her. Men were stupid. All of them, even her uncle for smiling at her as she rushed around the curve in the sidewalk. His smile slipped when he saw her.

"Good grief! Not you too." She plopped in the middle of the seat and wrapped the blanket around her shoulders. "When he comes back, I need you to drop me off at the shop before taking him to the Grand Central."

"Okay, Kerri-berri."

She squirmed on the hard bench seat. The day suddenly felt much too long. She was exhausted but sitting battered her body as badly as walking had. All she wanted was to get home and lay down. Maybe soak in a very hot bath.

"On second thought, can you take me home instead?"

"Are you okay?" her uncle turned to talk with her. "Your mom told me about the arthritis."

Kerri sank farther into the blanket and wished Eric would hurry up. Her emotions felt as raw and jagged as her joints. "I'm tired and cold. Never a good combination lately."

"What happened with Eric?" he tried to sound casual.

"Nothing." Kerri couldn't even think of anything else to add. After a couple of days of possibility, she was right back to nothing. That wasn't entirely true. She still had the pain. And it was growing more intense.

"I'm sorry. He seemed like a nice guy." James turned back to watch the trail.

"He probably is." Kerri had to move.

She crawled back out of the ATV and tried to do a few stretches with the blanket still wrapped around her. She flexed her fingers, wiggling then bending and straightening them. She held the side of the cart and bent her knees. Every time she stood back up she wanted to cry.

"Do you want me to go get him so we can leave?" James asked.

"No, he can't take too long. There isn't much to look at." Kerri hoped not at least. Plus, she was determined not to look any weaker than she had to in front of him.

They waited ten minutes before Eric rounded the corner. Kerri sat in the middle of the seat, the blanket wrapped all around like a mummy, and waited. He took his time crossing the last few feet. She saw him pause, then he climbed in the front next to her uncle.

Good.

She rode in silence all the way home. Eric and her uncle made small talk, but the tension remained palpable. Kerri couldn't decide what was worse—having him close but acting distant or the fact she wasn't sure she'd be able to walk into her own house when she got there.

Luckily, her uncle pulled into the yard, right next to the two steps up the porch. He jumped out and helped her stand.

"Want me to—" he started to ask.

"No. Talk to you soon." Kerri kissed him on the cheek. She didn't bother to say goodbye to Eric. Let him believe whatever he wanted. She couldn't change his mind anyway. Instead, she concentrated on taking one step after the other. She counted it a win that she didn't lurch. It was a double win that she didn't look back in a desperate attempt to see his face one last time.

Then again, maybe it wasn't. She closed the door and swiped at the tears that ran down her cheeks.

9

*E*ric had never felt so tired in his life. The day had started so nice, but Brynn's words kept running through his head.

If it works out, you don't have to go through this alone.

She hadn't really said anything about money, or that Kerri needed him to do something for her. But if not, why hadn't Kerri clarified that?

"So you're staying at the Grand Central Hotel?" James interrupted his thoughts.

"Yeah."

They zipped down Spring Street. When they turned on Main Street, James continued. "Look, it's probably none of my business, but Kerri's my niece."

Eric almost groaned. *Here it comes.*

"She's dealing with a lot right now. I've never seen her lash out like she did today." He pulled up in front of the hotel but grabbed Eric's hand before he could get out. "All I'm saying is don't judge her on today. Give her another chance."

Eric nodded, not trusting himself to speak. A niggling

fear had crept its way through his anger. What if he had jumped to conclusions?

As soon as James released him, Eric hurried into the hotel. He walked past the cluttered seating arrangement in the lobby and up the wide staircase to the second floor. His room was on the third, so he walked down a short hall and up another set of stairs. He used the old fashioned key with the traditional large wooden key chain to let himself in.

The first thing he saw was a finished sculpture and two unfinished ones. Last night he'd finished the first one. Kerri gazed up at him with a face full of innocence and light. He'd done his best work in a year.

He picked it up for a closer look. The details had him expecting the face to blink up at him through her lashes.

Lies, all lies.

He wanted to smash it, but he couldn't. Liar or not, Kerri had become his muse. She had drawn this level of craftsmanship from him. If he destroyed it, would he ever be able to work again? He set the piece back down on the kitchenette counter, letting his hand cup the side of her face.

It felt wrong. Because of the smaller scale, her face didn't fit in his palm the way the real one did. The dried clay was rigid and cold to the touch. Eric couldn't help but remember how warm and soft Kerri's skin was when she turned into his hand after he smoothed her forehead.

It was going to be a long afternoon.

Eric spent the rest of the day sketching ideas for other sculptures. None of them were of Kerri. Some of them were quite good, and he relaxed. He could find other things to inspire him. A new muse, if need be.

However, a second look through the pile of new ideas revealed a connection he hadn't planned. Each new idea related back to Kerri. They were things they'd seen that morning, others depicted scenes from memories she'd shared. Her voice and descriptions had inspired images in his mind. Images that his hands were eager to create.

By the time night had fallen, he'd successfully pushed the reality of Kerri to the back of his mind, replacing her with Kerri the muse. Something intangible and distant. He ate downstairs in the hotel restaurant, knowing that he wouldn't run into the muse or any of her family down there.

It was barely ten when he fell into bed. Unfortunately, he couldn't sleep. Lying in the dark with nothing else to do, his thoughts focused on Kerri. Although he'd only known her for a week, she had been fun and easy to be with. Nothing about her had made him feel trapped or like she wanted anything from him. She had never asked him for anything. In fact, several times she had tried extra hard to put walls between them. Was that some kind of reverse psychology? Did she think that by playing hard to get he'd chase her?

Hadn't he decided to do just that before they ran into her friends? That must have been her plan from the beginning, but that didn't feel right either.

Kerri hadn't played hard to get. Not really. He'd seen the longing looks followed by one of resignation as she pulled away again. She told him she didn't want a boyfriend and then took considerable care to keep things as just friends between them. Maybe Brynn had been wrong. If that were the case, why hadn't Kerri explained it instead of running away from the conversation at the hotel?

He should have gone home to North Carolina instead of hiding in Arkansas. Then he wouldn't have met Kerri and found himself in this predicament. On the other hand, hanging out with her had been exactly what he needed. He had created art again. Things of beauty and depth that his

New York stuff lacked. There was emotion in the clay once more.

Eric sighed, wishing sleep would claim him. He'd promised himself he wouldn't let a woman play him ever again. Vanessa should have sealed that conviction, but his heart obviously wasn't sticking to the plan. Heck, he thought Kerri might be using him and he still wanted to see her more than anything else.

He crawled out of bed and turned on the overhead lights. If he couldn't sleep, he'd work. He unwrapped one of the unfinished heads. It was Kerri on that first day in Frank's shop. Her wide eyes wary, scared. Seeing it was like a punch in the stomach. She'd looked exactly like that for a split second on the trail. Then the hurt and anger took over.

How could she fake that?

What if she wasn't hoping he'd pay for her medical bills? He hadn't really given her a chance to talk about it during their walk. Instead, he'd accused her of being like Vanessa. His stomach somersaulted again. She had said he was like Steven. Who was he? What if Kerri had been hurt as bad as he had? That would explain why she kept pulling away from him.

Shortly after, Kerri had rushed off and he had waited as long as he could before returning to the cart. When he reached it, her nose had been red, her lips blue, and her eyes dull. It's like he'd managed to turn off her inner light. When they dropped her off she hadn't even said goodbye.

Eric returned to bed. He punched the pillow and tossed around some more. The quaint Victorian hotel had lost all its charm. The overly abundant florals and doilies were too feminine. How was he supposed to stop thinking about a woman in such a girly room?

He must have drifted off because he found himself

waking up with light seeping around the closed curtains. A quick look at his cell phone showed it was after seven.

"I should just talk to her."

Eric showered, ate some breakfast, and arrived at the Manning home by eight thirty. He felt a little silly, but he knocked on the door anyway. Kerri's mom opened it.

"Oh, Eric, come in," she whispered. Cheryl closed the door softly and pointed to the couch. "Have a seat."

"I'm sorry it's so early." He sat, feeling a little strange. Why was she whispering? "I really need to talk to Kerri."

"I'm sorry, Kerri isn't up yet." Cheryl twisted her hands in her lap, much like he'd seen her daughter do. "She's having one of her flare-ups. Yesterday must have taken more out of her than she let on."

Flare-ups? Disappointment coursed through him. What if he couldn't get Kerri to talk to him? Maybe he could get the information from Cheryl.

"What's wrong with Kerri?" The words slipped out before he could think about them. "I mean, what kind of flare-up are you talking about?"

Cheryl tilted her head for a moment. "She hasn't told you?"

"No, but yesterday one of her friends hinted I could pay for her medicine." Eric tried not to cringe at the exaggeration.

"Is that what this is all about?" Cheryl shook her head. "Kerri was so upset last night, but she wouldn't tell us what happened."

"Does she hope I'll pay for her whatever medicine she needs?" He had to know.

Cheryl's brow wrinkled, and she fairly glared at him. "Is that what you think? If it is, you don't know my Kerri. She's as proud as she is kind and won't even let her father cash out some of his bonds to help pay for it."

Eric thought about that. Just because she wouldn't let her dad pay didn't mean she wouldn't hope for someone else to do it. How would he know for sure?

"Maybe I should come back later to talk to her." Eric reached over for the coat he'd laid on the back of the couch.

"That's a good idea, son." Ken stepped into the room. "I don't know what's going on, but she's not in any shape to deal with it today."

He didn't smile, and Eric felt that he had offended the man somehow. Eric stood, ready to leave when they heard Kerri.

"Mom?" her voice drifted down the hallway.

Cheryl jumped up. "I'm here."

Kerri appeared with an electric blanket wrapped around her, the cord trailing behind. Her hair was a mess of curls, but it was her eyes that grabbed Eric's attention. Dark circles highlighted the pain she felt.

"Oh!" Kerri dropped a medicine bottle. "I didn't know you were here."

She moved slowly, bending down, reaching for the bottle. Her dad picked it up first.

"Did you need me to open this for you sweet pea?"

"Yes please." Kerri's gaze jumped to Eric then down to the floor. He watched her take a deep breath before looking back at him. "Why are you here?"

"I wanted to talk to you, but I can come back some other time." Eric found that his feet were rooted to the floor.

What was wrong? She looked like she hadn't slept in weeks. Her dad supported her by holding onto her arm. Cheryl took the pill bottle from Ken. All three of them looked sad.

"Sweet pea, do you want me to call Bob and cancel? I can stay here as long as you need me." Ken gently pushed some curls off Kerri's forehead.

"Thanks, Daddy, but I'll be fine. I want to talk to Eric, and you don't have to stay."

"Okay." Ken squeezed her, then turned to Eric. "Don't disappoint me."

Eric swallowed. How many times had his dad told him something similar? His dad would have been disappointed at how he'd acted the day before. A real gentleman would have put Kerri's needs first, whether he believed them to be real or not. He owed her an apology and a chance to clear the air. "Yes sir."

Ken hugged his wife before he left with one last look at Eric and Kerri. "Call me if you need me, sweet pea."

"I will." Kerri watched her father leave. She held her mother's hand. "I have chronic rheumatoid arthritis. It's moving fast, and there's nothing I can do about it."

Eric tried to catch up with the quick change in conversation. Arthritis? Wasn't that what older people had that made their hands hurt? He remembered how her parents had taken care of the little things at dinner. Tying her apron, massaging her arms. Kerri looked like she might pass out any moment. He didn't remember moving, but he found himself beside her, reaching for her arm.

"Do you need to sit down?" He led her toward the couch.

"Thank you, but I'd rather sit in the rocker by the fireplace." She pointed to show him where. "It's my new favorite spot."

Eric helped her sit. He watched her shift the pillows around until she was comfortable. Her mom had already flipped the switch on the fireplace, and heat spilled into the room. Arthritis didn't sound that bad. Painful, sure, but it wasn't life threatening.

"I don't get it; you're still young." He sat on the end of the couch closest to her.

"It's not what you think. I have an auto-immune disease that attacks my joints. It's early for me, so you can't see that anything's wrong. Eventually, I will lose the use of my hands, elbows, anything really with moving parts. I'll curl up into a spinster hag."

"No." Eric looked at her delicate hands clenching the edges of her blanket, then down at his own. He couldn't imagine losing the use of his hands. His entire life revolved around using them to create things. "I mean, how did this happen?"

Kerri glanced at her mom.

Cheryl squeezed her daughter's shoulder. "Let me get you two some hot chocolate."

"With extra whipped cream?" A half smile teased Kerri's lips.

"Of course." Cheryl left for the kitchen.

"Mom thinks whipped cream is the answer to every problem. The more you pile on the faster you mend."

"Do you agree with her form of therapy?" he asked.

"Wholeheartedly." She sighed again.

"Kerri, why didn't you want to answer my question?" Eric's stomach turned to acid. His imagination was running wild.

"I didn't want to hurt Mom's feelings. RA is often hereditary. She thinks it's her fault, but it's not. It's no one's fault."

"There's so much I don't understand. How can you be so calm?"

Kerri did a strange little laugh sob thing. "Calm? You think I'm calm? Trust me, I haven't been calm for months."

She rocked the chair harder than needed, her fingers gripped the armrests. It was clear she didn't feel calm inside.

"Is that why you've kept this from your friends around town? People asked questions yesterday and you didn't share any of this with them."

She shrugged. "What's the point? It's only going to make them feel sorry for me. I don't need that." Kerri sighed and leaned back in the chair. "Can we change the subject?"

"Is it hard to talk about?"

"Yeah. Look, I'm sorry about yesterday. By the end I was tired, hurting, and confused. When you started yelling, I just yelled back. I shouldn't have."

"It's not your fault." Eric leaned closer, relieved they were making progress. "I should have let you explain. I'm listening now."

"Okay." Kerri blinked back some moisture that gathered in her eyes. "First, I never expected anything from you. Not a," she blushed, "relationship, or any help with my medical needs. Brynn is a closet romantic, but this is my problem and no one else's."

Eric watched her face. She looked sincere, but he still couldn't be sure. He wanted to believe, but he didn't know what to say either. Kerri played with the edge of the blanket. She'd looked him in the eye when she spoke, but as the silence grew longer she studied the seam. She appeared vulnerable and lost. He really hoped it wasn't an act, because if it was, he was still falling for it.

"So, Brynn just wanted someone to be your friend? Help you through this emotionally?" Eric finally spoke.

Kerri shook her head. "I don't know, but she doesn't really understand how my life has changed. I have no delusions that someone is going to come in and fix this."

"Has it changed a lot? Does that have anything to do

with Steven?" He hated the pain that flashed across her face. "You mentioned him yesterday."

She looked up to the ceiling for a moment before looking his way again. "My life will continue to change because of this disease. It's already caused me to leave school, and I won't be looking for a job any time soon. Before I came home, I had a boyfriend. He had our whole life planned. Everything was perfect. At least I had convinced myself it was, and then I got my diagnosis." Kerri shrugged. "He—"

A sinking feeling punched Eric in the chest. He watched her close her eyes, take a deep breath, and shake it off. Even though she looked broken, she was strong. Not only did she have to deal with the grim prospect of losing the use of her hands, but then her boyfriend had rejected her because of it. The tears didn't fall, and when she opened her eyes they were clear and determined.

"It doesn't matter. My life is not at a place where I can entertain ideas about anything other than day-to-day things right now." Her voice grew stronger. "Just know that I'm not stupid enough to think a complete stranger would do something my boyfriend of two years wouldn't. And no I didn't ask him, he made it clear he wasn't willing to continue our relationship down a path that would have made his help an option."

Two years? The man left her after two years? At least Vanessa only wasted eight months of his life.

"I'm sorry. Sorry that he was stupid. Sorry that I jumped to the wrong conclusions yesterday. It's just that people have used me for lots of things. I shouldn't have assumed you were too, but it's an easy jump for me." Eric was relieved when her expression softened. "Can we start again as friends?"

*K*erri's insides churned. Could she be friends with him? She'd never been so embarrassed in her life. He really had thought she was trying to trick him into paying for medicine or something. The only way he'd believe she wasn't after his money was for her to tell him about Steven. If she'd been making a list, that would be another mark against him.

1. He wasn't staying forever.
2. He didn't trust her.
3. He made her relive the whole Steven mess.

Other than that, he was almost perfect. Kerri sighed. If only she didn't feel so tired and sore, maybe she could think straight. As it was, knowing he didn't run because of her illness made her want to sit with him all day.

"It would be nice to start again as friends." Kerri gave him a sad smile. "Let's agree that's all this can ever be."

Eric nodded. "Okay."

Cheryl returned with a tray of cookies, a glass of water, and three large mugs full of hot chocolate. They were piled high with whipped cream and chocolate drizzle. A peppermint candy cane rested inside for stirring.

"Here we go." She sat on the couch and passed out the cups.

"This looks wonderful. Are you sure you don't want to sell food at your shop? This would be a huge hit." Eric warmed his hands on the side of the mug.

Cheryl laughed. "That would be something."

"Thanks Mom." Kerri took her pills with the water then reached for her cocoa. "Shouldn't you head to work too?"

"I do need to get the Mardi Gras necklaces done today, but I'm taking you to yoga first, per doctor's orders."

"When did you talk to him?" Kerri asked.

"Just now. Then I called your aunt. She promised the new guy would stay after his class and give you a one-on-one session at ten today." Cheryl quietly swirled her candy cane until all the whipped cream was mixed into her drink.

"Yoga? I've never done it myself, but I had some friends that loved it. It's supposed to help?" Eric took a sip of his cocoa. "This is really good Mrs. Manning."

"Thanks. It's supposed to help her joints. Dr. Dahler has been trying to get her to attend classes since before Christmas. Kerri however, refuses to give it a try."

"Mom, I have my reasons."

"What? It's not money, because you know Valerie won't charge you."

Kerri looked from her mom to Eric and back to her mom. She could feel the heat creeping up her cheeks. "I'm not flexible, and I don't want to look stupid."

Eric laughed. "That's the reason I'd give too."

"You don't have to worry about that. Valerie said it would just be you and the instructor. He'll know about the RA, so there's no need to be embarrassed."

"Just go to work, Mom. Sleep will help me more than anything else." Kerri drank her chocolate, feeling wonderfully warm inside and out.

"Eric, what do you think. Is she too stubborn or what?" Cheryl appealed to the man beside her even though he tried to hide behind his chocolate mug. "Seriously, if you were in pain, wouldn't you do anything it took to feel better?"

Kerri cringed. *Mom would have to put it that way.*

"Uh, sure." He looked from one to the other.

"You guys don't understand. It takes so much energy to move, how am I going to exercise? Let me sleep. I'll feel better tomorrow. Then I'll do yoga some other time." Kerri stood and tried to drag the rocking chair across the floor.

Eric jumped up. "Where do you want it?"

"The other side." She sighed. Had he really forgiven her, or was he just being a gentleman?

He moved the chair, adjusting it until she nodded her head in satisfaction.

"Thanks."

Cheryl stood. "I give up. I'll go to work, but you should reconsider. Your aunt wants to help. This is something she can do, and you need to let people back in."

After grabbing her empty cup, Cheryl headed to the kitchen. Kerri could hear her rinsing and loading the dishwasher. She felt bad that she'd upset her mom, but it all seemed like too much work.

"Kerri?" Eric watched her. "I know you don't want to, but it is okay to accept help when it's offered."

"I know, I know. It's just, I don't want to depend on others for everything. It starts with them donating yoga classes, and my parents moving my room downstairs. Even though it doesn't seem like a lot, they've rearranged their lives for me. It's not supposed to be like that."

"I see. You think you're a burden." His brow arched upward.

Kerri's heart stuttered. Was he sad for her, or was it pity? She automatically rubbed her arms, and the blanket slipped off her shoulders. Before she could pull it back up, Eric drew close and did it for her. He didn't scoot back to the couch but pulled her to standing. Once again she could feel his warmth.

"Yes." She whispered. *Wait, what am I saying yes to?*

Eric stood with the edges of the blanket still in his

hands. "Let me take you. We could talk some more while we wait, and if nothing else, it will make your mom feel better."

Kerri couldn't think. He was so close she could smell his aftershave. She just wanted to soak it in a little longer.

"Why?" Her voice sounded throaty to her own ears, but all she could do was stare into those wonderful eyes and wish she was healthy. Wish she could chase this man and make him love her. The thought rattled her even more. "Why are you being nice again?"

"I thought we were going to start over as friends?"

She inhaled a shaky breath. *Friends.*

It didn't feel like enough, but it would have to do. Could she be his friend if he started dating Brynn? The thought pushed her into panic mode. Her body shook with the need to flee, but he held her tight. One hand moved up to caress her face. He was so warm. So gentle.

His gaze drifted to her lips just like they had at dinner. That felt like a lifetime ago. Her body didn't respond like a friend's would.

She needed to get away. "I should get dressed."

"Are you going to go?" Her mom hurried back into the room.

Eric dropped the edges of the blanket and took a couple steps backward. His face looked flushed, but that was probably because of the fire.

"Eric said he'd take me, so I'll give it a try." Kerri pulled the blanket tight.

"Put on something loose and easy to exercise in." Her mom rummaged in the drawer of the entry table. "When you're done, come by the shop and tell me how it went."

Kerri sighed. "If it makes me more tired, I'm coming home to sleep."

"Okay, I'll trust Eric to take good care of you." She winked and walked out the door.

"It's like she lives on another planet." Kerri finally allowed herself to roll her eyes.

"Why's that?" Eric's dimples appeared.

"No reason." Kerri waved her hands around. She turned off the fireplace. "I'll be back in a few minutes."

She hurried down the hall to her room, leaning against the door once she'd closed it. The way Eric had held the blanket and tugged her closer made her sizzle. For a man so opposed to serious relationships, he sure sent some mixed signals. The need to reach out and touch him scared her. *Please don't like Brynn.*

Kerri dressed quickly in a snug t-shirt and yoga pants. She'd never used them for yoga before, but they had always been her first choice for winter exercise gear. After pulling her hair into a ponytail, she grabbed another bulky sweater for warmth. "That's as good as it's going to get."

She grabbed a lighter afghan from the bed to wrap around her while they waited to leave. Eric still sat on the couch sipping his cocoa. She glanced at the space beside him. *The chair is safer. Sit in the chair.*

Her legs had a mind of their own. She sank into the soft cushions of the sofa.

"How many blankets do you have back there?" Eric scooted forward to touch a tassel. He didn't move back as far as he had been when she sat down. "Tell me about what you studied in college."

"You don't want to know about that. It's boring business stuff. Numbers, spreadsheets, marketing plans." Kerri tried not to lean closer to him.

"Well, why did you choose that if you think it's boring?"

She shrugged. "I guess I thought it would come in

handy. I could help my parents with the shop or I could go out on my own."

"Were you good at it?" Eric took a drink, and when he pulled the mug away, he had a line of whipped cream across his upper lip.

"You've got a mustache." Kerri's laugh died on her lips the moment her fingers brushed his face, the cream disappearing under them. "I'm sorry. I didn't mean to…"

Eric grabbed her hand and kissed her fingertips. Heat and desire rushed through her. His warm breath caressed her knuckles as he whispered. "Thanks."

His voice sounded different. Lower, huskier. It thrummed all the way through her, and she couldn't move if she wanted to. She wanted to lean forward and taste the chocolate from his lips.

10

*E*ric didn't know what to do with himself. When Kerri leaned forward and wiped his lip, he'd almost fallen off the couch. She was so close. The blanket held open by her outstretched arms. It had taken every ounce of control not to lean in and join her in the circle of fabric.

Now she stared up at him, wistful hope shining in her eyes. She didn't smile, but he noticed her come forward a fraction of an inch. He'd never wanted to kiss a woman so badly in his life. In fact, he'd never been this affected by someone.

I've only known her a week. Shaking off his confusion, he forced himself back to his corner of the couch. Kerri glowed with the girl-next-door, steal-your-heart-forever kind of beauty. Was he ready for that?

He cleared his throat. "When should we leave?"

"Um," she turned to look at a clock on the wall behind her. "Ten more minutes? You know, I can always call my dad. I feel bad taking up so much of your time."

She was giving him an out. Again. That alone

convinced him. She had never wanted him to pay her bills. The strange thing was now that he knew she probably wouldn't accept it, he wanted to help her in some way. If she was this sweet sick, what would she be like pain free?

Slow down.

Unfortunately, his fingers reached out to touch a curl that had escaped her ponytail. He followed its silken length down to where it brushed the side of her neck. He'd add that little curl to one of his sculptures.

"No need. I want to help. Taking you to class is the least I can do. That's what friends do, right?" He watched her blink, nice and slowly. Was she as affected by his touch as he was by the warmth of her skin?

"Okay." Her voice was almost a prayer.

She jerked back at the sound of it, conflicting emotions flittered across her face. Eric gave her space, needing to keep contact, but knowing better than to scare her too much. They both needed more time.

"Why don't you tell me what you liked about growing up here?"

"Sure." Kerri curled her legs under her. Her gaze jumped from him to the room and back. "You'd think growing up in a place where everyone knows you would be rough, but I missed it while I was at college. It's hard when you need to explain everything to people. In little towns everyone already knows how you got that scar or who broke your heart in junior high."

"Who broke your heart in junior high, and do you have a scar?" Eric's curiosity couldn't be squelched.

Kerri just laughed. "See what I mean? I'm not telling you about my scar, and how do you know I didn't break all the hearts when I was younger?"

"Oh, I'm sure you did." He waved at the photos around the room. "I've seen how cute you were back then."

"As if! Most guys preferred to lavish their attention on Jen or Brynn, but that didn't bother me. Luckily, Jaya was so smart boys were scared of her. We kept each other company."

"Surely there was a guy or two that couldn't resist your smile?" Eric enjoyed the light flirting. It felt safe. Comfortable.

"Maybe one or two." She twisted the edge of the blanket in her hands.

"Did one of them break your heart?" He watched her eyes cloud over for a second before she shook her head. The hurt disappeared quickly, but he'd recognized the depth of her pain. He'd seen it enough in his own mirror after Vanessa dumped him. Did Kerri have that look because of Steven? Before he could ask anything more the phone rang.

"Just a minute." Kerri fumbled for the cell phone on the side table, knocking off a book and the remote in the process. Her cheeks flamed, and she kept her gaze on the floor while she answered. "Hello?"

She listened before saying, "Okay, thanks Aunt Val. We'll be there in a few minutes." After she hung up, she bent to pick up the stuff she'd dropped. "That was my aunt. She said we could come on over. They finished the class early."

"Where's your coat?"

"I'll be fine in the sweater."

Eric nodded. Kerri grabbed some keys and locked up as they left. Once they were in the car, he asked, "What was your favorite thing to do growing up?"

"I used to love roaming the woods and camping by the lake." She gave him a small smile, but her eyes didn't shine when she glanced at him. "I probably won't do that much anymore."

"Why not?"

"Look at me. One day walking around town knocked me out." She leaned her head into the headrest. "I need to accept I can't do all the things I used to."

"Your parents seem to think that isn't necessary." Eric thought about the conversation from their dinner several days earlier.

"They're counting on something that isn't going to happen." Kerri met his gaze. "Look, I know we've reached an understanding, but you hanging around will give my parents a false hope of another kind. There are things I need to accept, and there are things they need to accept. It will be easier for them if..." She shrugged and turned away.

Eric's thoughts tumbled over themselves in that confused way he was starting to associate with Kerri—surprise that she really wasn't trying to trap him in a relationship, hurt that she might not want to, admiration at her courage, and a longing to make things better for her. It made it difficult to keep his heart protected when he didn't know what was coming next.

"I thought we were friends?" he asked.

"We are. But even friends don't spend every day together. We should just plan on saying hi when we pass each other in town. Maybe chat at church potlucks. That kind of thing."

Eric tried to watch her and the road at the same time. She had stared out the window the entire time she spoke. Did she really want what she described?

"That sounds more like acquaintances than friends, and I don't know which church you go to. What if I end up at the wrong potluck?"

"Don't be silly. Thanks though." That little smile almost reappeared.

"For what?"

"For trying to make this easier." Kerri sighed. "You might not think so, but this is for the best. For a while anyway. If it helps, I'll miss you."

"You will?" He couldn't help but grin.

"Of course I will. You make me laugh, and not much has done that in a while. Turn here. Aunt Val's studio is right there." Kerri pointed to a building across the street. "It's on the second floor. You'll want to grab one of those parking spots."

Eric pulled into a spot and raced around to Kerri's side of the car where she had the door halfway open. "Hey, remember, opening doors is my job."

"I should do it if we're just friends."

"Nope. Guy friends can still open doors and hold their girl friends hands if they want. No complications, just," he shrugged, "nicer than not doing those things."

Kerri let him take her hand and help her out of the low seat. "That didn't make any sense, but whatever. Come on."

"Let me put the money in the meter." Eric's phone buzzed with a text. He almost ignored it, but habit won out. A quick glance showed it was from the Realtor.

The owner accepted your offer.

What? He had forgotten all about buying a house. Last night he would have said no way, but now he wasn't sure. Sliding the phone back in his pocket, he decided to sit on it. There were still papers to sign, so he'd play it by ear.

"Your aunt owns this place?" He had almost missed it, since the ground floor was a bar. Tucked to one side was a set of stairs leading up to a door. Someone had written messages about dance on the sides of the steps.

"Yep. She runs it with her husband. They've been trying to expand their services. Yoga is new. I don't know the guy they hired for that. He didn't grow up here." She took a deep breath and barreled up to the door. He watched her turn a key and step through. "Come on, I have to lock it back or it'll swing open."

Once she'd done that, they walked up another set of stairs to a sliding door and a little foyer. An older woman with streaks of gray in her dark hair came around the counter.

She pulled Kerri into her arms. "It's so good to see you. Monsieur Jarrod is waiting for you in the ballroom."

"Are you taking French lessons?"

Her aunt laughed. "No, but Jarrod is French and oh so handsome."

"Okay, I don't know why that makes a difference. Aunt Val, do you really think this will help?"

"It doesn't hurt to give it a try. Jarrod's really good at what he does. He trained on the East Coast before moving here. We're lucky to have him." Valerie directed her gaze to Eric. "Who's your friend?"

"Oh, this is Eric Hunt. I'm surprised Mom didn't mention him."

Valerie laughed. "Well, maybe she did. Come on." She ushered them through another sliding door into a spacious ballroom. The floors gleamed in the light from the windows. The overheads had been dimmed and soft spa-like music played. She whispered in Kerri's ear, but Eric still heard. "If it doesn't work out with this guy, maybe you'll consider Jarrod?"

"Aunt Val." Kerri rolled her eyes.

A fit, blonde-headed man in loose fitting pants and no shirt walked over and kissed Kerri on both cheeks. "You must be Kerri. I'm Jarrod." His French accent made his name sound more like *zsha-rod* than Jarrod. "I'm glad you decided to give yoga a chance. I'll help you relax."

He winked, and Kerri rubbed her arms.

She glanced at Eric before answering Jarrod. "I'll be honest, I'm not into this kind of thing."

"No worries." He smiled at her and spread his arms as if trying to give her the best view of his abs and chest. "Give it one try and see how you feel afterward." Jarrod recrossed his arms and flexed his muscles when he turned his attention to Eric. "And who might you be?"

Eric resisted flexing his own muscles but just barely. "Eric Hunt."

He held out his hand, but the yoga instructor ignored it.

"I take it you're not joining us." The guy scowled at Eric's jeans and sweater.

Before Eric could say anything, Kerri piped up, "He didn't know we were coming."

Eric relaxed as she turned her glowing face toward him and rested her hand on his arm. Who cared if this guy was posturing. Kerri would ride home with Eric, and he'd make sure she knew he wanted to spend more time with her.

Jarrod placed his hand on Kerri's elbow, pulling her away. "Let's get started. Your friend can wait outside with Valerie."

"No thanks, I'll hang out in here." Eric waved toward the sidelines. "There's plenty of space."

"Suit yourself." Jarrod smirked and led Kerri away. "Come to the middle of the room."

Eric found a chair in the corner. He pulled it by the long mirrored wall and sat down to watch.

"Do you plan to leave the sweater on?" Jarrod asked.

"Oh no. Just a minute." Kerri turned away from the man

and slowly pulled the sweater over her head. Her fingers caught on the t-shirt, giving Eric a glimpse of her abs before she brushed it back down. She looked to be in good shape. Her waist was as slender as he'd imagined. No fat, just smooth creamy skin. Eric pushed back the burst of desire as she carried the sweater to him. "Can you hold this for me?

"Sure thing." *Sure thing? Next I'll be offering to hold her purse.* Eric took the shirt from her outstretched arms. He resisted smelling it and sat down to wait, grateful she hadn't brought a purse.

Jarrod grabbed two mats and spread them out on the floor. "Valerie said you were sore and tight, so we'll keep it simple to help relieve the tension. Next time we can try some harder poses for balance and strength. Watch first, then I'll help you deepen the stretches." Jarrod sat on the floor. "First we'll do a spinal twist, like this." He modeled the pose. "Now you try."

"That's easy." Kerri sat on the mat. She moved her arms and legs into the same position Jarrod had.

"Good, that looks good." He moved over and ran his hand down her back. "Keep your back straight, good. Now breathe deep, in and exhale." He moved his hands to her shoulders, twisting her a little more. Then he touched her chin, turning it the opposite way from her body. "Keep your neck long."

Eric clenched his jaw when the guy let his hands linger in the corner where Kerri's neck met her shoulder. They moved through several more poses. The guy was all over her. It's like he searched for reasons to touch her, run his hands along her side. She had turned bright red, and she wouldn't look Jarrod in the eye.

"You have great muscle tone in your arms." Jarrod squeezed her arms in several places as he moved down her body. Eric couldn't understand every word the other man said, but his flirtatious tone was obvious. Jarrod's hand rested on Kerri's hip. "Do you feel the tension here as well as your back?"

Kerri winced and squeaked. "A little."

Eric jumped up. Flirting was one thing, but now he had caused Kerri pain. He was halfway across the floor when they noticed him.

"Yes?" Jarrod arched an eyebrow.

"Kerri, are you okay. If he's hurting you—" Eric found he had fisted his hands.

"It's a little uncomfortable, but I'm okay." She beamed up at him from the floor, sending his thoughts in all kinds of inappropriate directions. "Thank you though."

"Let me know if it's too much."

"It's my job to push her to her breaking point. That's the only way she'll find relief." Jarrod leered up at him as well, his hand rested on Kerri's shoulder.

Eric gritted his teeth at the blatant innuendo spewing from the yogi's mouth. Kerri must have noticed the tension.

"How much longer will this take?" she asked.

"Are you in a hurry, *mon cheri*?"

"No, but I don't have all day either." Kerri glanced at Eric.

He hoped she wasn't trying to rush because of him. He'd have to try harder not to let his feelings for Jarrod affect her. "Kerri, take your time so you'll feel better. I just don't want him causing you pain."

She smiled up at him, and the whole room seemed brighter.

"Good, good. Why don't you let us get back to work then." Jarrod waved him off. "Okay, I have another stretch we can add to the routine that will stretch the hip flexors better."

Jarrod continued to place his hands on Kerri. Each time, Eric wanted to storm over and rip off his arms. He tried to look away, but his eyes remained glued to the two of them. Every moment he wished it were his hands becoming familiar with Kerri's slender body. Several times, Jarrod slid his hands down Kerri's arm or leg and then smirked at Eric. By the end of the session, Eric stood with his arms crossed, glaring at the obnoxious instructor.

"Let's do child pose to end. You'll find it very relaxing." Jarrod purred as he stood behind her, gently folding her body over so that her head got closer to the floor. "Extend your arms outward, good. Don't forget to breathe."

He glanced Eric's way one more time before sliding his arms from Kerri's shoulders all the way down her arms to hold her hands, effectively covering her body with his. Jealousy growled through Eric. The gratuitous body contact had gone too far.

Eric stormed to their side. "Time to go."

"Careful." Jarrod moved away from Kerri. The jerk winked at Eric. "You don't want to destroy the peaceful calm she's found."

Kerri stood and looked up at Eric through her lashes. Her cheeks were flushed, and there was a slight shine to her skin. She reached for Eric's arm but dropped her hand before touching him.

"I'm sorry this took so long." Her eyes looked sad.

Eric hated that he'd made her feel like a burden again. All he'd wanted was to get the yoga guy's hands off of her. He took a few deep breaths of his own. It had never bothered him when guys touched other girls before. "It's okay. I wanted to make sure he didn't over-do your first visit."

A tiny smile teased the corner of her lips, and the depths of her caramel gaze stole his breath. The need to bend down and kiss her shook him to his core. He wanted to stake his claim, leaving Jarrod no doubt about her availability. Kerri blinked and the moment passed, but the ache in Eric's heart grew a little stronger. Right then and there he decided. He'd buy the house and chase this beautiful girl until she let him catch her.

Jarrod cleared his throat. "Today was good. Will you be back on Monday?"

Kerri startled as if she'd forgotten he was there. "Um, I'll think about it."

If Eric had anything to do with it, Kerri would only come to the scheduled classes from now on. Better yet, he would buy her a video she could do from home. *Get a grip, man. This is not your choice.* But he wanted it to be.

"You know where to find me if you need anything." Jarrod led them out the door and back to the lobby. "And I do mean anything."

Jarrod stepped forward as if to hug Kerri, but Eric was ready.

"Let me help you with your sweater." Eric cut the other guy off and gently placed the sweatshirt over her head.

Kerri giggled as she poked her head through the opening and moved her arms into the sleeves. "You'd better be careful. I could get used to a southern gentleman taking care of me."

"How about a Frenchman?" Jarrod asked.

Kerri looked up at Eric as he pulled the shirt down the rest of the way. "No, I think I'm a strictly southern kind of girl."

Eric's heart soared. Was she finally flirting back? He

could have stood there looking at her smile all day. It didn't hurt that Jarrod scowled in the background.

Her aunt approached, breaking the spell. "How did it go Kerri?"

"I'm tired, but better." She gave her aunt a hug. "How much do I owe you?"

"Nothing, don't be silly."

"Aunt Val, you have to let me pay." The pretty pink blush crept up her neck.

"I'll square it with your mom later. Now get out of here and enjoy the gorgeous day out there. We're supposed to get snow next week." Valerie waved them toward the door.

"Thanks again, Aunt Val." Kerri reached for Eric's hand but stopped at the last moment.

He liked the way she kept moving to touch him, and even if she didn't follow through, he could. She turned to lead the way out, and Eric reached for her hand. It was soft, delicate, and fit perfectly in his.

She gazed up at him with those wide eyes. "I really do feel better. Thank you."

"How about we get some lunch?"

"Sounds wonderful." She gave his hand a little squeeze.

At the door, Eric turned to see Jarrod watching. The caveman inside sent the yogi a big smile and a nod towards his hand clasped with the beauty beside him. *Take that Mr. Hands.*

11

K*erri* couldn't believe the words that had slipped out of her mouth. *I'm a southern kind of girl*? Ugh! However, Eric was now holding her hand, so maybe it wasn't as stupid as she thought. His hands were as strong and warm as ever. She hated the fact he'd have to let go when they reached the car.

However, Eric paused before opening her door. "So what did you think of your first yoga lesson?"

Kerri dipped her head to hide from his gaze. It was so intense! "It was as embarrassing as I thought it would be. I promise, I do know how to follow instructions."

"What do you mean?" one of his brows arched upward.

"He kept correcting me like I was five. Always shifting my shoulders or the tilt of my head. All he had to do was tell me what I needed to change." Kerri huffed as she realized it wasn't her fault. Jarrod had simply assumed she didn't know what to do and took matters into his own hands. She glanced at Eric, surprised to see a huge smile on his face. "What?"

"You have no idea, do you?" He spoke soft and low.

"About what?"

Instead of answering, Eric laughed and opened her door. "Do you have a favorite place to eat?"

Before she could answer, he reached across her body to buckle her in. He moved in slow motion. All ability to think melted with his warmth. She heard the click of the belt, and then he brushed his way past her. He stood in the door looking down at her like he was waiting for something.

What did he ask? Oh, yeah food. "I guess it depends what you're in the mood for?" She swallowed as his gaze dipped slightly to rest on her lips. Every inch of her warmed, and her mouth went dry. *Yes, please.*

"I'd like to celebrate." He half grinned, half smirked before pushing himself away from her door. Did he know what she'd been thinking?

Once he was buckled in, Kerri asked, "What are we celebrating?"

"Exactly one week ago, I walked into your shop. Meeting you was perhaps one of the luckiest things that has happened to me in a while." He reversed out of the parking lot and headed down the street. "Where to?"

"Oh? Park at your hotel and we can walk to Local Flavor. You can't go wrong there, and it might not be too crowded yet." Kerri smoothed her sweater underneath the seatbelt. Her heart still clipped along at a faster than normal pace. "Why do you think meeting me was lucky?"

Eric glanced at her, then back to the road. "Lots of reasons, and I hope to show you over the next few days."

Her breath caught in her throat. That could mean a lot, or it could mean nothing, and she couldn't decide which way she wanted it to go. Finally, she forced herself to think of him. To put him first, but her voice trembled slightly. "As friends right?"

He frowned for half a second, before nodding. "Of course. You have no idea how much I needed a friend I could trust to show me around town."

Kerri relaxed a bit. She could do this. She could be his friend. Eventually, she'd stop staring at his hands and hoping they'd touch her. Then she'd stop looking at his lips and wishing they'd lean close enough to slide against hers. She brushed those thoughts away and tried to concentrate on the conversation.

"Surely you had friends in New York?"

He shrugged. "I had a lot of acquaintances. All of them needed or wanted something from me—a seat at an exclusive restaurant, tickets to one of the galleries, an introduction to another *friend*." He said the word with derision. "It got to the point I didn't want to be around anyone."

"So that's what you meant by always being used. Is that why you're in Eureka Springs?" Kerri watched him drive. His hands were steady, but his brow was wrinkled as if he were in pain.

"Yeah. I guess you could say I ran away." He turned down Main Street toward his hotel. "I'm getting pretty good with these winding streets."

"You do seem to know your way around."

"I like it here. It reminds me a lot of home, but smaller."

"Why didn't you go home?"

"I probably should have." He pulled into a spot, turned off the car, and twisted in his seat to look at her. "But if I did, we wouldn't be celebrating right now."

Kerri felt her face and neck growing warm again. All thoughts of safely keeping their relationship as friends faded. Could she really take a chance on being happy? Just for a little while?

"How long do you really think you'll stay in Eureka

Springs?" she asked breathlessly. Would a couple of months be enough?

Eric reached out and held her hand in both of his, rubbing one of his thumbs over her palm. Kerri stopped breathing all together.

"I found a house."

Kerri inhaled so fast she almost choked. "What does that mean?"

"It means I like it here. There's lots of," he lifted her hand, turning it to kiss her palm, "potential."

Lord, help me, I don't have a chance!

"Eric?" Kerri startled at the way his name had slipped from her lips with such longing.

She was about to pull free when he tugged her forward. He held one hand, his other ended up on the side of her face, gently guiding her closer. He paused, hovering just above her lips. Kerri ached to close the rest of the distance, but he spoke before she could.

"Kerri, would you give me a chance?" His breath caressed her face, warm with a hint of peppermint from their earlier cocoa.

In answer, she gave in to the magnetic pull she'd been fighting for days. She strained against the seatbelt, leaned forward, and touched her lips to his. It was sweet, simple, and everything she needed. His hand entwined itself in her hair, holding her close. The other hand moved to the other side of her face, tracing along her jaw line, then down her neck to rest on her shoulder.

She wanted to wrap her arms around him and drag him to her side of the car, but she didn't. Instead, she pulled away and looked up into his face. Her heart raced with hope and fear. He was everything she'd ever wanted, but could she trust that? When things got hard, he could move on as easily as Steven. He'd already run away from New York.

Eric left his hands resting against the side of her face. "You look scared. I shouldn't have kissed you." He moved away and got out of the car.

Kerri slumped in her seat. *Why do I have to mess everything up?*

She turned to open the door, but Eric was already there. Ever the gentleman, he offered her his hand. Once she was out, she held on tight, not letting him pull away.

"Eric, wait. I am scared." Her neck and cheeks grew even warmer. "There's so much you don't know about me, about my condition. I look at you and I forget everything until it crashes back on me."

"You do?" he stepped closer.

Kerri nodded and tried to catch her breath.

Eric wrapped his arms around her and asked, "Why do you forget?"

"Um." She breathed him in, feeling weak in the knees. Goodness he smelled good! And his arms were warm. "I...don't know?"

He chuckled. "I like when you're evasive. It makes me want to convince you to trust me."

"I do." With the words came the realization that she really did trust him.

"Is that what scares you?"

"Maybe."

"We'll take this slow then. There's plenty of time to figure out what this," he waved between them, "is."

Kerri could only nod in response. No guy had ever been this considerate, and she'd dated many nice guys over the years. She let Eric lock up the car and then they walked hand in hand down the street toward one of her favorite restaurants. Even though she wasn't hungry, she knew exactly what she'd eat. That's if she could swallow anything at all. Eric had a way of filling her so full she didn't need anything else.

~

*E*ric loved how Kerri's hand felt in his. After he kissed her, she looked terrified. He thought he'd messed up his chance, so he got out of the car. The entire time he strolled around to her side he mentally prepared himself to take a step back. Give her room. However, when he opened the door she had held on to him.

Now they walked side by side down the street. She trusted him. Eric couldn't help but smile as he squeezed her hand. She looked up at him in that special way she had that made him feel like he'd come home. Maybe he needed to concentrate on this look for another piece in the series. Then he'd have three to go along with the full body one he'd started on Tuesday.

"What are you thinking?" she asked.

"A lot has changed since this morning." At her frown he pulled her closer and wrapped his arm around her shoulders. "I'm sorry I didn't believe you. Even more sorry that my behavior yesterday probably contributed to your pain this morning."

He felt her shrug.

"It makes sense though, because of what you experienced in the city. I'm sorry people used you like that."

"I shouldn't have assumed you were like them. I knew you weren't from the moment I met you, but—" Now it was his turn to shrug.

"It doesn't matter now. Tell me about the house you're going to rent. Where is it?" she asked.

Grateful for the new subject, he talked while they crossed the street. "It's not far from your house on Spring Street."

"I didn't know there were any rentals open on Spring."

"There aren't. I decided to buy."

Kerri's steps slowed until she pulled them to a stop. "You're buying a house in Eureka Springs?"

He nodded.

"Why?"

"Why not? It's a good investment, and if I stay, this house will allow me to get exactly what I want."

"Wait, there's only one...you're buying the cabin close to the grotto! Oh my gosh. I can't believe it." She clamped a hand over her giggles. "I'm sorry. Some of my friends and I dreamed about that house when we were teens."

"Have you ever been inside?" He followed her up a few stairs to enter the restaurant.

"No, but I always wanted to." She waved at a woman behind the hostess stand. "We passed it all the time whenever we walked to the grotto. It always looked so homey and comfortable."

"Kerri. It's good to see you." The woman picked up two menus. "Just the two of you today?"

"Yes ma'am." She answered.

"Oh stop. You're making me feel old." She led them across the room into an area full of tables. Everything was close and cozy. Someone had decorated the shelf around the top of the wall with all sorts of different lamps. Eric didn't see any that matched. He liked it. "Here you go. Do you want your usual starter?"

Kerri turned to him. "Do you like brie cheese?"

"Sure. Order whatever you want." He loved the way her eyes sparkled in the softer light of the restaurant. Her smile lit up the whole room. Heck, if she kept looking at him like that he would order everything on the menu if it made her happy.

"You'll love this." She cocked her head to the side. "Well, I hope you will."

He couldn't help but chuckle. "I'm sure I will."

They took a few moments to go over the menu and order. Eric enjoyed the comfortable silence while they considered their options. He could easily imagine working in his new studio while she curled up on the couch with a book. Yeah, he'd have to put a couch in there.

It didn't take long for their appetizer to arrive. The same woman brought it just a few minutes after they'd placed their entree order.

"I thought I'd get this out before we get swamped with the lunch crowd." She set down a large platter with baked brie in the middle, surrounded by some kind of honey sauce and sliced pears. "Tell your folks I said hi."

"Thanks, I will." Kerri waited for the woman to retreat before grabbing a fork. "You've got to try this, but let me warn you, if you touch anything on my side you are dead." She proceeded to cut the cheese in half, pulling hers closer.

"Is that so?" He reached across the table and stabbed at one of her pears.

Kerri laughed and used her fork like a sword in an effort to protect the cheese from his attempts to steal it. "No fair." After a few more failed attempts at defense, she switched to offense and snagged a huge bite from his side. "This is my all time favorite." She licked a drip of honey from the side of her hand.

"I can see why." He tried not to watch every move she

made with those lips, but time after time his gaze drifted to their sweetness. *I shouldn't have kissed her.* He really needed something else to concentrate on. "Hey, did you ever make a decision about the chocolate thing your parents mentioned at dinner?"

She set her fork down. "No, not really. It's probably too late anyway."

"Maybe not. Do you want to do it?"

"I don't think so. I love making chocolates, but the thought of running my own shop doesn't excite me like it used to." She pushed a pear around the plate. "If only there was some way to get paid for making them without worrying about orders and delivery and everything else that goes with a business."

Eric savored another bite of the warm cheese, thinking about what she'd said. She liked making them but didn't want to be tied down to orders. It sounded a lot like why his art had started suffering. Once he created things based on orders, he lost the joy. She was an artist at heart and needed a way to stay true to that.

"You look serious all of a sudden." She leaned forward. "Want to share?"

"I might have an idea. You like the creating part, right?"

"Yeah."

"You also said you started it with your friend?"

"Jen. We would get together Sunday after church and make as many goodies as we could to sell through the week." She twirled a lock of hair around one of her fingers.

"How often did you make them alone?"

He watched her bite her lower lip in concentration, and he ached to take over the job for her. Then she sat straighter in her chair.

"I've never done it by myself. Not even the ones you had.

My friend Mic came over and we spent the morning catching up while we made them." She paused again, looking around the room. "I can't imagine doing it by myself."

Mic? Eric wondered why she'd never mentioned him before. He pushed the sudden jealousy away. She needed him to focus on the chocolate problem, not his need to make sure every guy in the state knew Kerri was his. Or she would be, as soon as he could convince her.

"Not that I couldn't do it myself. It just wouldn't be as much fun." She returned her gaze to him. "How did I not see this?"

"See what?" he encouraged her to keep talking it through.

"It's the experience I love. I'm creating, but I'm doing it in a social setting."

The waitress interrupted them by refilling their drinks.

"Amazing truffles is just a by-product then."

"You're right. Maybe I should start a video channel like Mic." She tilted her head to the side in thought.

There was Mic again. "Who's he, and does he make money at that?"

"Huh?" she mumbled it around the food in her mouth. "Sorry, Mic is a high school friend. Oh, there he is now."

She stood up in time for a fluffy haired guy to swing her around in a hug. "I thought that was you. Getting an early lunch?"

"Yeah. Mic, this is Eric." She left her arm around his waist but turned to make the introductions.

Mic slid his arm from Kerri's shoulder and held out his hand. "Nice to meet you. Kerri mentioned she was going to show you around. How do you like our little town?"

Eric tried to watch all the visual cues in an effort to

figure out if Mic was really a friend or something more. Kerri appeared comfortable hugging and touching him, but she had already sat down. If they were involved, would she have stayed by his side? Mic smiled. Did he realize Eric was sizing him up?

"If you're not careful, you could fall in love with this place." Mic winked.

It felt more like a shared secret than a challenge. Eric's shoulders relaxed. "I think I'm well on my way."

"Good. This town," Mic cut his eyes toward Kerri without looking at her, "deserves all the attention you can give it."

"Agreed." Eric nodded.

"What's with the cryptic guy talk? You both sound silly." Kerri scooped up the last of the brie with her pear. "Do you want to join us, Mic?"

"No, I'm coming to help in the back for the lunch rush." He hugged her in her chair. "If I hurry, I can make your meal just the way you like it."

"Don't let me keep you then." She laughed and shooed him away. Eric watched her swirl her finger through the honey and lick it off. "I should have made him take the plate."

"He seems like a nice guy."

"Mic is the best. He's like the brother I never had, and he's always been there for me." She played with her napkin as she talked.

"You never dated?" he tried to sound casual.

Kerri screwed up her face. "No way. When I say he's like a brother, I really mean that."

Good. Eric relaxed into his seat. What had they been talking about before? "He has a video channel?"

"Oh yeah. I think he does pretty good with it. Last I

checked he had five or six hundred thousand subscribers, all tuned in to watch him cook." She shook her head. "Who knew?"

"Maybe you could do that. Don't sell chocolates. Sell the experience of making chocolates."

"That really would be a dream job, but would it feel like I'm doing it alone if I'm just videoing it?"

Eric thought about it for a moment. "You could set up a shop front with the kitchen right there for everyone to see. Customers would schedule time slots to come make truffles or whatever. You demonstrate and teach, but they do most of the actual work. That would make it easier when your hands hurt. Also, people could watch from the window, or come inside to listen. It would be advertising while the customer is making the treats."

"Would people pay to do that?" she asked.

The waitress brought their food to them, but Eric didn't start eating right away. "They do stuff like that all the time. Pottery, painting, other kinds of cooking classes. Why not a chocolate class?"

Kerri jumped up from her seat and practically fell in his lap trying to hug him. He stood to make it easier. He didn't even care that the restaurant had filled with people. It simply felt good to hold her while she shivered in his arms.

"Kerri?" he didn't want to let go, but he wasn't sure if she was crying or not.

"Thank you." There weren't any tears in her eyes.

"What for?"

"For giving me hope and a plan. I can do this. It feels right, exciting."

"You're welcome then. Glad I could help." He scooted over a chair and had her sit in his. This was much nicer than having her across the table. "Let me get your food for you."

"I'll take it home. I'm not really hungry." She squeezed his hand in hers. "You eat though."

"I can take mine to go too."

"My mind is on hyperdrive now, but my body is so tired from everything. Would you mind us going back to my house to finish?"

"I'm sorry, I should have considered that." Eric looked around and waved down their waitress to ask for to-go boxes and the bill.

"No way you could have. I would have made it through lunch, but now I want to sit with a notepad while you eat. I can start outlining a business plan." She sucked in a quick breath. "Could you stay for a while to help me think it through?"

"On one condition."

"What's that?"

"Come see my house when I get the keys." He watched her eyes light up even brighter.

"Really? You'd let me check it out?"

"I'd love to hear your opinion on my plans for it."

"I don't know what you get out of this, but deal."

12

*K*erri couldn't help but smile as she dressed for the day. After their Thursday lunch, Eric had spent the afternoon with her. She had curled up in one corner of the couch with a blanket and notebook while they discussed how to make a viable business out of her showing people how to make chocolate. When her hands and wrists started hurting, he had massaged them quite thoroughly. The kisses that followed had been an extra bonus.

He stayed for dinner with her family. It was just as wonderful and easy as that first night. Even though he sat across from her at the table, she still felt him beside her. They didn't talk about her RA or the misunderstanding of the day before. Instead, they shared the business model with her parents. Kerri couldn't remember a happier time.

They spent all Friday afternoon hanging out too. She took him back to the Crescent Hotel where they ate pizza and took selfies in front of haunted room 218. Ever since he decided she wasn't trying to use him, he was back to his flirty self. He was always finding reasons to hold her hand or lean in for a quick kiss.

And when they weren't together, she thought about him constantly. Today he would move into his new house and she'd finally get to see inside.

"Kerri, breakfast is ready." Her mom called down the hall.

When she reached the cheerful kitchen, Kerri was surrounded by the yummy smells. Her mother pulled a pan out of the oven with something yellow and green in it. Closer inspection showed multi-colored peppers, spinach, eggs, and cheese.

"What is this? It smells delicious." Kerri bent over and breathed it in.

"I tried a new recipe from the book Dr. Dahler recommended. You know, that Mediterranean diet book." Cheryl pulled out plates and served up the casserole. "This is an egg and spinach frittata."

Kerri gave her a hug. "Thanks Mom. This is great."

"I'll be trying lots of new things for you."

"You don't have to do that. I should learn to cook this stuff for myself."

"Maybe we can do it together. Your dad and I need to start eating a little healthier too." She patted her stomach. "I'm getting rounder and slower every year."

"Whatever." Kerri took a bite of the eggs. A burst of flavor mingled with the eggy goodness. "Oh my gosh! This is delicious. Sit down and eat with me."

"Sure, tell me what you and Eric are doing today." Her mom sat down with her own plate.

"He's getting the keys to his house, so we're going to check it out."

Cheryl clapped her hands. "I still can't believe he picked one out so close to us."

"Don't get any ideas, Mom."

"What? I've seen the way you light up around him, and you haven't mentioned Steven once since you met Eric."

Kerri couldn't deny that. "Eric is a major upgrade from Steven."

"We agree. Especially since you two worked out whatever happened the other day." Cheryl finished her breakfast and started cleaning up. "When is he picking you up?"

The doorbell rang and Kerri laughed. "Right now."

"See if he's had breakfast." Cheryl retrieved another plate while Kerri answered the door.

"Hey." Kerri admired his dimple. She wanted to kiss it as part of her hello, but she couldn't bring herself to do it. "Mom wants to know if you've eaten yet?"

"Morning, beautiful." He bent down and kissed her on the nose, making her sigh with delight. "I could always eat more."

His greeting and touch thrilled Kerri down to her toes. She pulled him inside. "Come on then, she made something new and it's fantastic." They ate and laughed with her mom and dad. Kerri still couldn't believe how well he fit in with them.

She decided to ask him about it when they were in the car for the short three minute drive to his new place. "How do you do it?"

"Do what?" He glanced her way.

"For a city slicker you fit in really well here."

"Ah, well, remember I'm not from New York City. I only lived there for two years. My hometown is much smaller. We have about fifty thousand people."

"Really? That might be smaller than Fayetteville."

"Is that where you went to college?"

"Yes. No wonder you get along so well with everyone."

Eric laughed. "And I thought it was my charm."

"Maybe it's the southern gentleman trait that's ingrained in you?" Kerri stopped talking as they pulled into the drive. This was one of the few houses with plenty of parking space. She stared at the warm wood on the outside of the house. The yard was gray and a tad overgrown, but she could remember times when it had been gorgeous.

"Do you like it?" Eric opened her door.

"I've always liked it. Something about it has always felt like home, you know?" She couldn't believe she was going to see inside. "I'm glad you're buying it."

Eric opened her door and helped her out of the low car. "Do you want to see inside the main house first, or the guest house?"

Kerri felt the pull to the main house. That was the part she used to dream about when riding her bike past it. "Can we do the main house first?"

"Of course." Eric pulled out a key chain with several keys and a tag on it. "We just have to figure out which key fits."

Kerri laughed. "It'll be an adventure."

Eric tried three different keys before the door clicked open. Kerri took a deep breath and stepped inside. It wasn't what she had imagined. The floors were beautiful wood, and even though the walls were a bland neutral, she could envision it full of color. A stone fireplace took center stage separating the living room from the kitchen but still leaving an open feel to the space.

"What do you think?"

"Look at the doors." She pointed to the crisp white barn style doors. "It gives it such character."

"I agree." Eric took her hand and led her to the kitchen. "I want to update the kitchen without losing the charm. Could you help me redesign it? I want the best. One that any cook would be happy to be in."

"I'd love to help." Kerri soaked it all in.

The kitchen was small, but it wouldn't take much to make it functional. She even liked the green cabinets. Kerri looked around again, trying to get a hold on her run away emotions. She really was glad Eric was moving here, but part of her was sad that she'd have to let her dream go. This would be a place she could visit, but it would never be hers.

"What are you thinking?" Eric stood beside her, his smile warm, familiar.

"I'm wondering what the upstairs looks like." She flicked the hair off her neck and shoulder before turning to the stairs. "And the guest house. You still need to show me the guest house."

"Let's go." He showed her around, talking about his plans for each space as he went.

Kerri could see everything thing he described. The hard part was she kept placing herself in the scene. She could see herself cooking in the kitchen while he sat and talked to her. Or cuddled up on a couch in front of the fireplace. Kerri tried to tamp down her runaway thoughts. There was no way he'd choose her. Not when he could have any girl he wanted. He probably had several perfect women lined up in New York waiting for him. Even if he enjoyed being with her now, eventually he'd return to that more glamorous life.

Eric continued talking about ordering furniture online and locally. "Maybe I can find some pieces around town to round it out. Kind of that vintage look."

"I'm sure you could." Kerri followed him to the guest house.

"I can't decide whether I want my studio upstairs or down. There's great light in both rooms."

She watched him pace back and forth before doing the

same upstairs while he tried to decide. He was as excited as a kid at Christmas.

"I'll have to think about it some more." He stopped wandering from room to room to look at her. "You're probably bored."

"No, I'm really not. This place is even better than I thought it would be." She swallowed the lump of sadness and concentrated on how happy he was. "No matter what you decide, this is going to be amazing."

"I can't remember the last time I was so excited about something. We need to celebrate."

"I know what we need." Kerri knew what she needed anyway. A distraction. "We need to make something dipped in chocolate."

"Really? You'd make treats with me?" He stepped closer and pulled her into a hug.

Kerri blushed. If he only knew. "Of course."

"I'm all in. Then you can help me search for furniture that will fit my new home."

~

The short drive back to Kerri's house was fairly quiet. Eric had noticed Kerri battling her emotions during the house tour. It was obvious she liked the house, and her enthusiasm for his ideas matched his. Then he caught her looking around with such longing on her face. That was followed by the resignation he'd seen many times. He knew that feeling often related to her illness, but how did it relate to his house?

Kerri had pasted on a smile and responded appropriately to his conversation. The clues to her real heartache lay in her body language. She often touched random things like doorknobs, the rail on the stairs, the cabinet handles, and even the window sills as if she were trying to memorize them. Several times he caught her looking at him with the same longing. As she grew more solemn, Eric had grown more hopeful. Yes, Kerri loved the house, but chances were just as good that she was falling in love with him too.

He would show her how he felt by finishing his sculptures in time for Valentine's Day. That meant he would have to work every day from here on out. But today, he'd enjoy every moment with her and his only goal was to make her laugh.

Eric pulled into her narrow drive. "Do you have everything we need?"

"Of course. If we got snowed in we'd run out of soda, but we'd have chocolate to last a week." She reached for the door handle.

"Wait, haven't I trained you yet?" Eric unlatched his seatbelt and reached over to grab her hand. "What do I have to do to keep you still while I walk around the car?"

She settled back in the seat and looked up at him with those expressive eyes that begged him to kiss her. "I don't know?"

He released her arm and cradled her face in both hands, ignoring the gearshift digging into his side. "If you sit very still," he leaned down and whispered against her lips, "I'll open the door and do a more thorough job of this."

His lips pressed softly to hers. He had planned to move away after that brief contact, but instead he nibbled on her lower lip. Kerri's arms came up around his neck as she melted into him, returning the kiss. He moved a hand into her hair, loving the soft curls. She was so warm. Her lips parted, inviting him in.

Eric didn't know how long they sat there, entwined and

lost to the world, but he finally pulled back to rest his forehead against hers. "Do you know how hard it is to stop kissing you?"

"If it's half as hard as letting you stop, I might have an idea." The sound of her voice was a caress against his cheek. "You'd better come open my door."

"Yes ma'am." Eric moved away slowly, but then he raced around to her door. Kerri waited for him, only sliding out when he helped her. He closed the door, then backed her against the car. "I believe I promised you another kiss."

She curled into him, sliding her hands up his chest to rest on his shoulders. One hand moved until she placed a finger on his lips. "I don't think friends kiss quite like this."

Eric felt like someone had dumped cold water on him. After all the little kisses of the past two days, she was pulling away again. And yet, she still nestled in his arms. It was as if her body and words were telling him two different things. She needed more time. He determined to sneak a kiss or two if she'd let him, but for now he'd play along.

"You're right. I bet you've never kissed Mic like that."

"No." She shook her head at the thought. "I don't think I've kissed anyone like that."

He watched the blush creep up her neck to her ears, glad that little tidbit had slipped from her sweet lips. Yes, the chase was on. He wanted more from and with her.

"Come on, let's get you in where it's warmer." Eric wrapped his arms around her and walked her up the porch steps.

Once inside, they hung their coats by the door. Kerri led the way to the kitchen where she proceeded to boss him around like a pro. She had him melting chocolate, stirring concoctions, using a tiny ice cream scoop to form fillings, and generally having a great time.

"I think these are ready to dip." Kerri checked a batch of the raspberry cremes he had enjoyed so much that first night. She pulled them out of the fridge and set them on the counter. "Bring that white chocolate over."

He did as he was told while she set a clean tray under the drying rack. She was adorable in her frilly apron with snowmen on it. He had learned she had a collection of aprons for every holiday and season. Standing in her kitchen he knew without a doubt he wanted to see her in every one of them.

"Eric?"

"Sorry, what was that?" he needed to stop fantasizing and pay attention.

"Are you bored?" Kerri placed her hands on her hips, but she had a gleam in her eye.

"No, far from it. Why?"

"Because," she walked toward him. He didn't see the spoon in her hand until she reached up and painted a white chocolate stripe down his nose.

"You didn't." He couldn't believe it. His serious, tempting muse had a playful side. He didn't bother to wipe it off. "You're going to pay for that."

"Oh yeah?" Her eyes twinkled as she grabbed the bowl. "You appear to be unarmed."

He stalked toward her. She retreated one step at a time, her smile growing larger with each one. At the end of the counter she flicked the spoon his direction. Chocolate splattered across his face and apron. He lunged. She squealed as she dashed around to the other side of the island.

Eric took a moment to look around the kitchen. She had the only bowl of chocolate still soft enough to smear. That meant he had to catch her before he could exact his revenge. He chuckled as the cliché *sweet revenge* entered his mind.

He chased her halfway around the island before pivoting back to catch her as she rounded another corner. She turned her back to him in an effort to keep the bowl out of his reach. Eric wrapped his arms around her, making sure she couldn't get away. Her warm body squirmed against him. It set him on fire. He tickled her side and managed to get the spoon out of the bowl.

Kerri giggled. "Don't, please don't. I promise I'll be good."

"You sure will." He shifted her in his arms until she faced him. Then he smeared chocolate on her cheek. She turned her head, getting some in her hair.

"Eric." She laughed and put her hand in the bowl.

It dripped as she placed it on the side of his face. Instead of turning away, he turned into it, licking the chocolate from her fingers.

"Oh!" Kerri dropped the bowl, but neither of them cared.

He continued to clean her fingers with his tongue while she molded her body to his. The counter was at his back. A hard contrast to her warmth. He lowered her hand to his chest and moved in to kiss the chocolate on her face. Kerri made a little moaning sound.

"Is it okay if I kiss you now?" Eric whispered.

Kerri didn't speak, but she nodded.

After several minutes of intense kissing, Eric let her go. "I'd better leave."

"Why?" Kerri gazed up at him.

Her lips were pinker than normal from his kisses. The sight of them made him want to dive back in. She still had candy coating on her face and in her hair. He touched a chocolate curl, pulling the strand straight, smudging even more chocolate.

"Eric?"

"Because all I can think about is kissing you."

"Oh." A little smile turned up the corners of her mouth.

It was her temptress look. The one he wanted to label as the 'I didn't know I could do that to Eric' look.

"Sorry to bake and run, but," now he retreated to the other side of the island, "I'll see you at church tomorrow."

Eric turned and hurried to the front door, hoping she hadn't noticed her physical affect on him. The cold air helped clear his mind. However, it didn't change his mind about Kerri. She was the real deal. The woman he'd always hoped to find but didn't think he would.

Yes, coming to Eureka Springs had been the best decision he'd ever made.

13

_____

Kerri's cell phone woke her from a dream about Eric. He'd been holding her close, asking her if she loved him as much as the house. She sighed at the wishful thought. Her phone rang again. She fumbled around until she found it under her pillow.

"Hello?" She tried to forget how nice Eric smelled, how much fun it had been to make truffles with him. The way his kisses melted her faster than the chocolate.

"Morning sleepy head." Jen's voice was muffled by the sound of the wind.

Kerri sat up. Her half asleep, muddled brain focused at her best friend's voice. "You heading to class?"

"Yep. Did you forget about me?"

"What do you mean? We talked two days ago."

"Yeah, and you didn't mention anything about a certain someone you've been seeing a lot of."

"It's only been like a week or so. Who told you?" Kerri sagged against the pillows. "I wanted it to be a surprise."

"It doesn't matter who told me, but I want details!" The

sound of the wind stopped and Kerri figured Jen had entered a building on campus.

Kerri sighed with pure happiness. "He's wonderful. We've spent almost every day together this week and part of the week before. It's kind of crazy how it feels like he's always been here."

"Ooo, love at first sight? God, I wish it would happen to me."

"It will, one day. Anyway, who says this is love? We're like best friends."

"Who kiss? Please tell me one of us is getting some affection."

Kerri laughed. "Oh man can he kiss. I can't think when he kisses me, but then again, I can hardly think when he's close anyway."

Jen squealed. "Jaya, and now you. I'm so happy for both of you."

"You'll get to meet him when you come this weekend."

"Good. Which brings me to the second reason I called. Are we going to enter the Chocolate Festival? Please say yes."

"Jen, why do you want to enter? Is it what you want, or what you think I want?" Kerri heard Jen sigh again.

"Would you believe me if I said it's what I wanted?"

"Not really. You grew out of our chocolate phase a long time ago. You don't even eat it anymore."

"Kerri, I'd do it for you. I can tell you don't love your major, so I hoped to push you back to your original dream."

"You don't have to do that. I'm not sure what I want to do yet, but I've been thinking about it and if I had my own shop, candy making would become a job. That would take all the joy out of it." Kerri chewed on a fingernail while she waited for Jen's response.

"But it was sort of a job when we were in junior high. What would be the difference?"

"Insurance, a lease, utilities, equipment, supplies, marketing, just to name a few. I like sharing my treats with friends and family more than selling to strangers."

"I can see that, but you need something that will make you happy." Jen was talking fast, a sure sign class was going to start soon.

"What if I told you that I still need your help at the chocolate festival, but not as a contestant?"

"Wait? I thought you didn't want to do the festival."

Kerri laughed. "I know you need to get to class, but I do have a plan. It's something Eric helped me come up with, and I'm excited about it. I'm not sure if it's what I want either, but it's worth giving a try just to see how it works out. How about you call me tonight, and I'll tell you all about it?"

"Deal! You sound so happy. I don't care what it is, but you can count on me."

"Hugs. See you soon."

"Hugs!"

After Jen hung up, Kerri stretched again. She'd been so wrapped up in having fun and enjoying every day that she hadn't had time to feel sad or dwell on her aches and pains. They hadn't disappeared, but they were bearable now that she had something else to look forward too.

"Knock, knock." Her mom stuck her head in the door. "You have a guest."

"It's not even eight yet." Kerri jumped up and searched for clean clothes. She definitely needed to do laundry today. "Tell him I'll be a few minutes."

"Will do. He said he doesn't plan on staying, but he brought something for you."

"What?"

"I don't know." Cheryl smiled. "Your dad is sitting with him."

"I'll be quick." She hurried into her bathroom to change, hoping her parents were behaving themselves. She pulled her hair up in a ponytail and splashed some water on her face.

As she entered the living room, both her dad and Eric stood up. She could tell that pleased her dad. He patted Eric on the shoulder before excusing himself.

"Have a good day sweet pea, and I'll see you tonight." Her dad hugged her tight and whispered in her ear. "I really like this one."

"Love you, Daddy." She hoped Eric hadn't heard.

Turning to him, she noticed he hadn't shaved that morning. His scruff begged for him to put on a plaid shirt and chop wood in the backyard. "Hi."

"Sorry to come by so early, but I thought you might want this." He held out a thin wrapped package in the shape of a DVD.

"What is it?"

"Open it." He ran his hand through his hair. Was he nervous?

She carefully tore the corner of the wrapping and pulled back a strip of paper to reveal a yoga DVD. She couldn't hold back the laugh.

"This is great, but what made you think of it?" she asked.

Eric shifted from one foot to the other, his hand still rubbing the back of his neck. If she didn't know better, she'd think he was blushing.

"I wanted to make sure you could do yoga anytime you wanted. This way you don't have to wait for a class or appointment." His words didn't quite match the level of his discomfort, but it didn't matter to Kerri.

She stepped forward and gave him a big hug, crushing the video between them. "Thank you."

His arms encircled her waist. "Plus, I—" He stopped mid sentence and shook his head. "Never mind."

"What? You have to tell me now."

"It's silly." He squeezed her tighter and let her go.

"Will you tell me one day?"

"Maybe, but I'd better go. I really want to finish my project so I can show it to you this week." His confidence returned with a show of his dimple. "It might mean I don't see you for the next few days though."

Kerri felt the sadness of that possibility tug at her. She tried to shrug it off. "I need to finish a paper anyway if I want to graduate on time."

Eric reached up and touched her cheek. "You are amazing. I'll think about you all day."

Kerri's mind blanked out like it always did when he touched her. All that mattered was the warmth of his hand on her face, the depth of his gaze, and the distance between them. Even after a couple of days hanging out, most of them ending with kissing, she still got nervous about closing that gap. She didn't want to scare him away, but she craved being close to him.

Luckily, he stepped closer, his fingers traced her cheekbones, her eyebrows, her lips. They were gentle as they explored every little detail of her face. When her knees weakened, he lowered his lips to hers. Tasting, questioning. She went up on tip-toe, wanting to give him the answers she couldn't speak out loud.

"Oh!" Her mom's gasp finally broke the spell. "I'm sorry."

When Kerri whirled around, she only saw her mom's retreating back. A silly smile took over. Well, now her mom knew Eric had kissed her. She turned back to see him watching her closely.

"Thank you for the video. I think I'll try it out today."

He visibly relaxed. "You're welcome. I'll text every time I take a break."

"I'll look forward to it, and I can't wait to see what you're working on."

His hands traced her face again. "I hope you'll like it. It's something from my heart."

"Then it will be wonderful."

He simply nodded. "I'd better go or I'll stay all day."

Kerri giggled. "Go then." She walked him to the door where he kissed her knuckles before running to his car.

14

*K*erri hadn't seen Eric in two days, but they had texted several times. She knew he was working hard in his new studio. She could walk over and see him, but she had promised she wouldn't. He had been super secretive about whatever he was working on. They had been playing a guessing game through texts that bordered on ridiculous at times.

Her favorite guess was he was sculpting the guy that fell off the scaffolding in the Crescent and died in what would become room 218. It was her favorite because Eric had proceeded to detail what such a sculpture would look like, making her laugh until her sides hurt. She loved that he could do that without being in the same room.

Kerri sighed. How could she be so completely in love with this guy so quickly? *Whoa.* Was she really in love? Before she could think about it her phone rang.

"Hello."

"Hey, Kerri, it's Frank. Are you free tonight?"

"Sure, what do you need?"

"Nothing. Eric will pick you up at 7:30 and bring you to the shop. We have something to show you."

"What is it?" Kerri hated surprises. Well, only when she had to wait all day for them.

"Can't tell you right now, but I'll see you tonight." Frank hung up.

"Well." Kerri shook her head. She couldn't remember Frank ever hanging up on her. He must be really excited. That made it harder to focus on her homework, cleaning her room, and double checking that she had the supplies for her first chocolate demonstration. The festival organizers had agreed to let her set up a booth in the lobby of the convention center on Saturday. She'd be the attention grabber for those coming into the event.

The afternoon moved along quickly. She helped in the shop, wondering at the fact Frank's store was locked tight. Kerri rode home with her mom and was sitting with her in the kitchen when Eric knocked on the door. Funny how she had learned to recognize his knock already.

"He's early." Kerri's heart pumped double time.

"He's always earlier than he says. It's like he can't wait to get here." Her mom grinned and pumped her eyebrows at Kerri.

"Mom, please." Kerri wiped her hands on her jeans but smiled like a fool anyway.

"I'll get the door." Her mother hurried away before Kerri could fuss more.

"Good evening." Eric breezed into the living room.

"Hi." Kerri almost squealed at the sight of him. He wore a red plaid button down that went deliciously with the day old scruff. *Finally!*

The only thing that would have made his entrance better was if he gave her a hello kiss. She shook her head and cleared her mind of that image. "What have you been up to all day?"

"Surprises." Eric didn't kiss her, but he took both her hands in his warm ones. "Frank said he'd meet us at his shop so you can see it."

"What is it?" Kerri's heart hummed and her skin tingled to the beat.

"I started a new series right after I met you. I worked all night and finished them early this morning. Frank's been helping me set them up in a display."

"You haven't slept?" Kerri noticed the rings around his eyes. It also explained the slightly thicker facial hair. She reached up to run her fingers along his jaw line. "I really like this look on you."

"You do?" He pulled her closer, then just as quickly pushed her away again. "Nope, no kissing. Not yet anyway. Frank is waiting for us."

Kerri laughed. "Not even one tiny one?"

"One is never enough." His words thrummed through her entire being. "Let's go so we can get to the kissing part."

"Shoes, she needs some shoes." Her mom hurried from the hall with Kerri's boots in hand.

"Thanks Mom." Kerri used Eric for balance and tugged them on. "I'm ready."

Kerri almost laughed at how excited Eric acted. He fairly carried her out the door to his car. His arms stayed around her, keeping her close. The car was even running, so it was warm when she slipped inside. Most importantly, a big grin never left his face. She allowed herself to get carried away with his enthusiasm.

"Are you going to tell me any more about these sculptures of yours?"

"We'll be there in another minute, so you'll have to

wait." Eric pulled into a parking spot at the top of the street. He opened the door and led her across the road where he knocked on the shop door. Kerri watched Frank walk through. He also had a silly grin on his face.

"Come in, come in." Frank pulled her into a hug. "You'll be the first person to view our new lower gallery."

"It's ready to open?" Kerri let them lead her to the huge doors that reached from floor to ceiling. They were already thrown open, revealing the flight of stairs going down.

"Wait." Eric stepped in front of her. "Close your eyes and take my hand."

"I don't know." Kerri felt a twinge at the thought of going down the stairs blind.

"I promise I won't let you fall." Eric's words pierced her heart.

Kerri looked deep into his eyes. The depth of his kindness and affection were clear to see. He'd never looked at her in quite that way before. The little aches that had pestered her that morning faded under his gaze.

"Okay," she whispered. Kerri let him take her by both hands and closed her eyes. He was a solid presence in front of her, guiding her carefully and slowly with his hands and voice.

"This is the last step, careful. Okay I'm going to turn you and then there is one more step down." He spoke softly, close to her ear. His breath moved across her cheek.

Kerri turned toward his voice, her face brushing against his lips. She froze, enjoying the tremor that ran through her. He had been much closer than she'd thought. Eric held still for a moment as well. Kerri heard Frank's steps as he descended the stairs.

"Are you ready to see what you've inspired?" Eric asked.

"Me?" she gasped.

"Yes, you with your courage and perseverance in spite of pain." Eric turned her a quarter turn and rested his hands on either side of her arms. "Open your eyes."

She slowly did as he asked, scared by what might await her. Three busts sat on a bar-height table. All were of her. She sucked in a gulp of air and moved closer. The first one showed her head bent in thought, a little crease of pain etched into her forehead, her hair was a riot of untamed curls. In the second one, the curls obeyed and lay in soft waves around her face. That face gazed upward through long lashes, her lips somewhere between a surprised O and pursed for a kiss. The last one had her hair up in a ponytail, one curl resting against her neck. Her face exuded such joy. She couldn't believe he'd been sculpting her all this time.

The details were so fine she thought she could be looking in a mirror. "These are amazing. How did you do them so quickly?"

She turned to Eric. His eyes beamed with pride and accomplishment.

"I've never worked so fast in my life. It's like I had to do them." He took a step forward. "Did you see the one on the floor?"

Kerri spun around. It only took two steps to walk around the table to see what had been half hidden behind it. She sat on the floor, huddled around a miniature space heater. A broken wing lay on the ground beside her, the other one bent and wilted. The sadness on her face so palpable that it hurt her for real. Kerri stared at the statue of herself from the first day she met Eric. Is this what he saw when he looked at her? A broken angel?

A sob escaped before she realized it was building. She didn't want to be his broken angel.

"Kerri?" Eric tried to reach for her, but she dodged and fled up the stairs.

"Go after her boy." Frank's voice faded as she reached the top and spun toward the front door.

Kerri knew she couldn't outrun Eric, but she didn't want to face this now. She couldn't hide the fact she'd fallen in love with him. How could she keep hoping for a future with him now she knew he'd never see her the way she saw him. She would always be the broken one.

She reached the corner of the road at the same time Eric caught up with her.

~

*K*erri stopped running under a street lamp. She was surrounded by a halo of soft yellow light. Her face stricken. Eric noticed she rubbed her arms furiously.

"What's wrong?" He tried to reach for her but she jerked away.

"Please, let me be." She sucked in another ragged breath.

"I don't understand. Tell me what's wrong." All his excitement had evaporated when she'd run away. Had she understood what his pieces meant? Did her tears mean she didn't return his feelings? How could he have been so wrong?

"I can't." She turned back to him. "There's so much to say, but I can't. It wouldn't be fair."

She doesn't care for me as much as I do her. The shock of it almost stole his breath. Frank had been right; he did need her like the air he breathed.

"Kerri..."

"I'm so sorry, but it hurts too much." Another tear slid down her face.

He couldn't lose her; he had to keep her talking. Maybe one day he could convince her to love him back. "Is it your hands?"

"No, yes. There'll always be something, but that's not what I'm talking about." She wiped her fingers across her cheek, then tapped her chest. "I broke my promise. It's not fair to you."

"What promise?" Eric's heart doubled with renewed hope.

"I promised myself. You deserve so much better." She rambled while she paced. "But it's too hard."

This time Eric managed to get his arms around her. He pulled her close and searched her upturned face, hoping she started making sense soon. "What's too hard?"

"Loving you, knowing you'll always see me as broken." Her voice hitched, and she tried to pull away again.

"You love me?" Now his heart soared. He picked her up and swung her around. "You love me."

She clung to him, the tears streaming down her face.

"Why do you think I see you as broken?" he thumbed away a tear as it slid down her nose.

"Your sculpture." She gasped for air between sobs, but she had finally stopped trying to escape. "The broken angel."

"You are an angel." He kissed the top of her head. "But you didn't look close enough. Her wings weren't broken. She was shedding them in order to stay on earth. As my muse."

Kerri made a little choking sound. "What?"

His fingers traced her cheekbone, down to her lips. It only took a second, but he'd wanted to do that for days. He'd missed her so much. Her smile, her light. "How can you not know how I feel about you?"

"How do you feel?"

He could sense her holding her breath. She didn't move when he bent closer and touched her lips with his. Her colder ones warmed as he wrapped his arms around her tighter. He could feel her hands balled up between them. They flattened against his chest as she relaxed into the kiss.

He willed all the words he wasn't sure how to say into that kiss. When he finally pulled away, she blinked up at him. A lonely snowflake drifted by. Then another. The light snow made everything feel magical.

"I've fallen in love with you too." He whispered into her hair. "You are strong and courageous. Every day you have pain, but you still smile and show everyone around you this beautiful light. Not seeing you for two days about drove me crazy."

"Oh." A shocked look flitted across her face. "Really? You could have anyone. Someone healthy."

"Shhh. You keep trying to save me from you, but you don't have to. No one else has ever made such an effort to put me first. Don't you see? We need each other." He didn't loosen his hold on her, afraid she'd slip away and run again.

"You need me?"

He caressed her face. "Yes. Let me prove it to you every day."

"Eric, I want to. You have no idea how much. But I'm scared. My condition is going to get worse. It may take a while, if I'm lucky, but it will happen. What then?"

"You don't have to be scared. I did my research on RA, and even though I don't know exactly how it will be, I know we can do this together."

She sighed and buried her face in his shirt. Her hands

gripped the fabric, and he thought he heard her breathe him in. "What about your career?"

"You've done wonders for my career. Do you realize that I've created more in the last two weeks than the last year? When I'm with you, I'm inspired by your spirit. Even when you want to give up, you don't."

"I've given up lots of times." Her voice vibrated against his chest.

"I haven't seen it."

Kerri's fingers tightened around his shirt again. "What if your feelings change? You've only known me for two weeks."

"It's enough to see how wonderful you are. To know how I feel when I'm with you."

"But—"

"Kerri, Frank was right. You think too much. How will we know if we're ready for more if you don't let me be with you now? I'm not asking for forever. Yet. I'm asking you to date me now. To see what we could have together."

"Oh."

He couldn't tell what that one word meant. She continued to rest against him in silence. It was becoming unbearable, but he would give her the time she needed. When she finally looked up, it was his temptress gazing at him. That hopeful smile, the chocolate eyes peeking through the long lashes.

"So you're asking me on a date using sculptures of my face?"

His joy rumbled out as a chuckle. "Was it over the top?"

"I don't know. Maybe I should look at them again before I decide. What if you used my bad side?"

"You don't have a bad side." He ran his hands up and down her back, happy with how well she fit in his arms. "Kerri, I'm not going to run away."

She nodded her acceptance. "I believe you, but what are you going to do when I get scared again?" There was a teasing quality to her voice. Her hands traveled up to wrap around his neck. "You might have to keep convincing me you're staying."

Eric laughed. "Challenge accepted."

The snow continued to fall, but Eric didn't notice. He was too busy convincing Kerri that a future with him was exactly what he wanted.

THE EUREKA IN LOVE SERIES

Read the rest of the stories from this cute little mountain town. Stories do not have to be read in order to be enjoyed but this is the suggested chronological order.

Chocolate Kisses by River Ford
Forgetting You by Hillary Ann Sperry
Landscape Love by River Ford
Teacher's Crush by River Ford (Coming Soon)
After the Fall by Tamara Hart Heiner

Other stories by River Ford
A Christmas Prayer (Previously part of A Merrily Matched Christmas 2017, Re-Released as a single—2018)
Christmas Magic (November 2018)

Get *My Brother's Best Friend* free when you sign up for her newsletter. Text NEW READER to 444999

ABOUT THE AUTHOR

River Ford is the romance pen name of science fiction author Charity Bradford. She lives in Northwest Arkansas with her family. She's always loved the Christmas and Valentine's special movies on the Hallmark channel. When she discovered the historic town of Eureka Springs, she was compelled to fill it with even more romance.

Join Charity's Street Team for the most up to date news on:

- New releases
- Sales and other promotions
- Giveaways and contests

- Opportunities to beta read and critique books before they're released to the public for free

Join Now— at https://www.subscribepage.com/eoeox8

amazon.com/River-Ford

facebook.com/RiverFordRomances

twitter.com/charitybradford

Made in the USA
Columbia, SC
16 March 2019